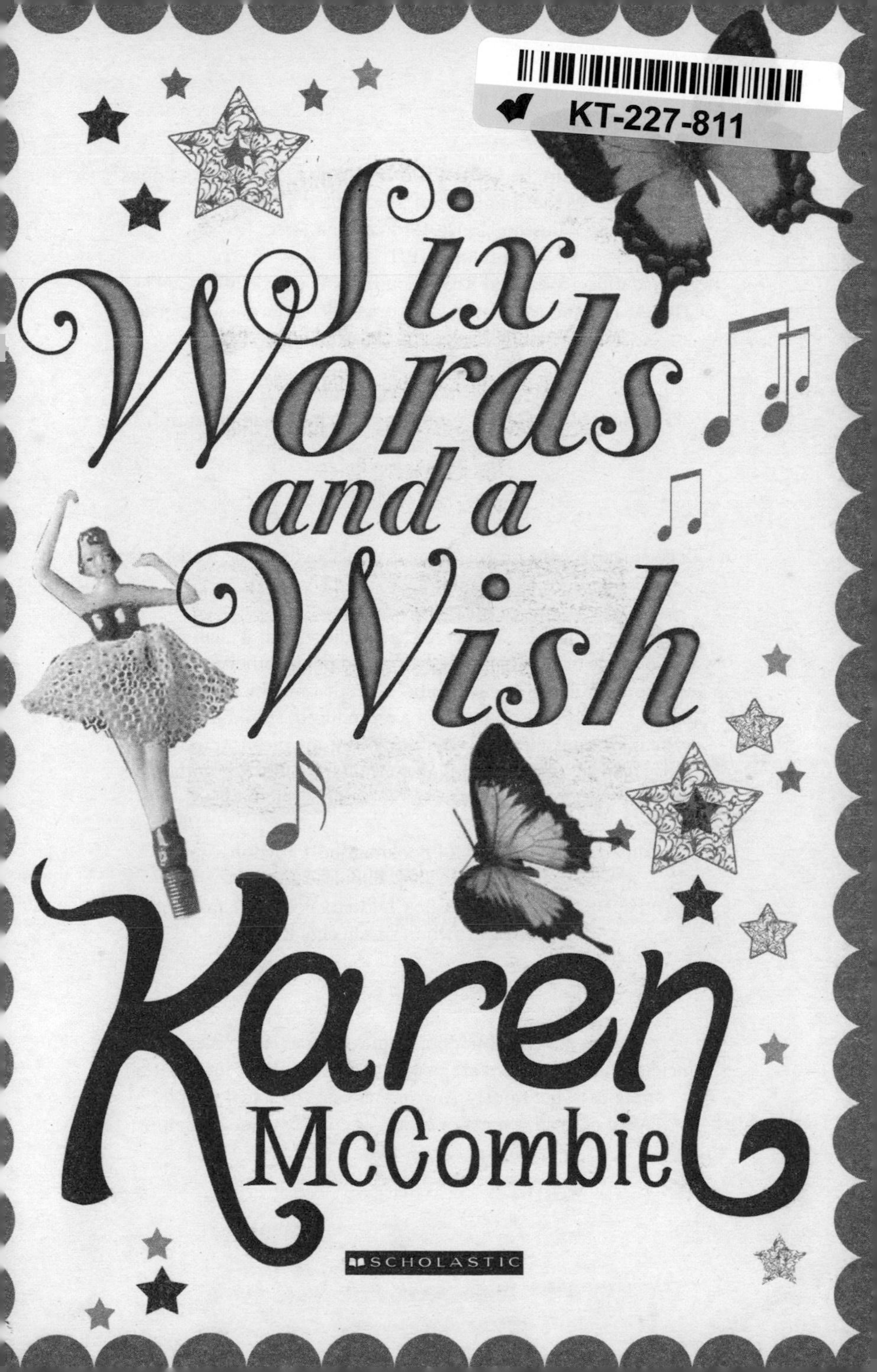
KT-227-811
Six Words and a Wish
Karen McCombie
SCHOLASTIC

First published in the UK in 2011 by Scholastic Children's Books
An imprint of Scholastic Ltd
Euston House, 24 Eversholt Street
London, NW1 1DB, UK
Registered office: Westfield Road, Southam, Warwickshire, CV47 0RA

ISBN 978 1407 10788 2

A CIP catalogue record for this book is available from the British Library.

Printed in the UK by CPI Bookmarque, Croydon, Surrey.

Papers used by Scholastic Children's Books are made
from wood grown in sustainable forests.

1 3 5 7 9 10 8 6 4 2

www.scholastic.co.uk/zone

For whoever lives at No. 32. . .

I Wish. . .

Can people explode?

With sheer, bubbling-under-the-surface rage, I mean?

It looks like Gracie might.

(*Tick-tock, tick-tock, she's a teenage time bomb and she's about to go off in this scuzzy, packed, ex-school-hall. . .*)

I've tried my best, I really have.

Just like everyone else around me (except Dolly), I came in here and sat down cross-legged (tough, when you're Dolly and you've got four legs to cross), ready to watch and listen to the lame show or performance or demonstration or whatever it is that Gracie's dragged us to.

But a few minutes ago, it all went a bit uh-oh.

That's cause these smiling, young, hippy-looking blokes wandered in with their African drums – and instantly switched their smiles for eyes-closed, trance-like head-wobbling as soon as they began badda-booming.

(The sniggers were a heartbeat away.)

Then I knew I was about to lose it for sure when one bloke with messy blond dreadlocks began making this endless gurgly, *droning* noise in his throat.

(The sniggers were bubbling up.)

That's not what got me, though; it was the fact that everyone around me suddenly began "ooh"ing and "ahh!!"ing and nodding appreciatively, as if the gurgly drone was a truly amazing vocal ability, rather than just incredibly *nuts*.

All at once, I got the giggles, badly.

Help – you know how it is; once you start, you just can't stop – a bit like finding your feet superglued to a runaway skateboard heading down a steep ramp.

And it's especially bad when you're somewhere you really *shouldn't* be giggling, with someone who is seriously going to kill you if you don't shut right up.

Don't! I try to order myself now, but myself is too hysterical to listen.

"*Jem!*" Gracie hisses at me. "Quit it!"

Her face is tense, a mix of anger and embarrassment.

(*Tick-tock, tick-tock. . .*)

Obviously, I know I should quit it, just like Gracie says.

But there's no button to switch off a bad case of runaway giggles, is there?

"*Jem!* Did you hear what I just said?!" Gracie hisses again, her grey eyes glowering at me like lasers, as if she wished she could instantly zap me into a pile of non-annoying dust.

(*Tick-tock, tick-tock. . .*)

A simple "yes" to Gracie's question is beyond me. I'm so lost in suffocating ripples of giggles that I can't even grunt out a vague "mmm!" in reply.

Uh-oh – now Dolly's joining in, with a strange kind of low-level, tuneless, whiny *yodel*.

I'm not sure if my stifled sniggering set her off, or the dreadlocked gurgler bloke.

Urgh. Even just *thinking* of him as the dreadlocked gurgler bloke makes me instantly worse. I'm in serious danger of choking – if my sister doesn't reach over and strangle me with her bare hands first. . .

(*Tick-tock, tick-tock, tick-tock, TICK-TOCK!!*)

Through the snigger-tears brimming in my eyes, I see Gracie flop her forehead on to the palm of her hand, the muscles in her face contracting with irritation.

I should pull myself together. I should clamp my

hand over Dolly's snout and whisper a small but genuine "Sorry" in Gracie's direction. I really should.

But the unstoppable ripples of giggles just keep rolling on and on. . .

"God, you're *all* the same."

It's barely a whisper.

But I guess that when you've grown up with someone, you can always tune into their voice, however quietly they're mumbling, however loud drums are drumming and dumb dogs are yodelling.

Gracie's latest darkly meant words work like a gloomy charm on me, my giggles stumbling to a standstill.

The thing is, I've heard this line before (lots of times), and I know the "all" she's wearily muttering about is Mum and Dad – and me.

"*None* of you take me seriously," Gracie whispers, tight-lipped, in the direction of her lap.

(*The tick-tocking's stopped. She's switched from explosive to implosive, like she wants to fold herself and her anger up into a tiny ball and disappear.*)

"Sometimes I wish–" my sister murmurs bitterly, but I jump right in before she can say another word.

"Look, I *know* what you wish, Gracie," I lean sideways and whisper tersely in her ear, my voice back in my control again. "Just for once, d'you know what *I* wish?!"

Gracie says nothing. She doesn't look up at me, she doesn't *explode*, she doesn't turn invisible.

So I carry on.

"I just wish—"

And I say the words.

And my wish comes true.

And I wish, wish, *wish* that it hadn't. . .

Chapter 1

Feeling a squeak

How dumb did I feel?

I was crouched down, listening to someone's *knees*.

"See, Jem? It's squeaking, isn't it?" said Iris, frowning.

I listened hard.

Really hard.

Just to make Iris feel like I was taking her and her squeaking knee seriously. Having a friend who's a hypochondriac requires quite a lot of patience. And imagination.

"I can't hear anything," I answered, with my face about three centimetres from her skinny jeans and the palms of my hands resting for balance on the pavement.

How did I end up here?

A minute ago we were having our usual post-school orchestra rant: the one about how naff the corny old rock classics that our music teacher, Mr Steed, made us work on were, and how we were both going to give it up and do something much, *much* cooler musically with our Saturday mornings. (Though what that cooler thing could be kind of stumped us. Round our way, thirteen-year-old-girl guitarists weren't exactly *swamped* with cool options for stuff to do.)

Then the next minute, Iris had stopped dead, and was staring down at her knee as if she'd never seen one of those before.

"Hmmm. Well, I can *definitely* feel it!" muttered Iris, now wiggling her leg around experimentally, and nearly clunking me on the head with the bottom of her padded guitar case.

"How can you *feel* a squeak?!" I challenged her, standing up quickly to avoid the clunking, which made the neck of my own guitar thwack me on the back of the head.

How dumb was *that*?

Like Iris, I've been playing guitar since I was seven and a half. Which means that for six years I've been walking to and from school (twice a week, since we joined the Saturday morning orchestra) with my backpack style guitar case and I *still* manage to thwack myself regularly on the back of the head.

I really should switch to playing the recorder. . .

"Ouch!" Iris winced for me, watching as I rubbed uselessly at the thwacked spot, ruffling my hair into a nice tangle in the process. "But hey, look, Jem! Over there!"

And so I looked, momentarily forgetting my thwacked head as fast as Iris seemed to have forgotten her squeaky knee.

Up ahead on the pavement was a woman I'd never seen before – with a small kid in tow – staring open-mouthed at my house.

They were new to the neighbourhood, for sure. Cause for people who've never stumbled across it, or are of an easily confused disposition, my house really is quite something. Not the place itself, I mean, since it's a pretty standard 1930s terraced house, same as all but one of the forty or so houses in our street.

So what exactly was making this woman gawp?

I guess it was the strands and strands of Christmas lights trailing from the roof, attached to the fence either side, pinned back like some giant spangly door curtain.

It was the fake snow in all the windows, and the half-size plastic reindeer teetering on its dainty hooves on the tiled awning above the front door.

It was the pudgy Santa Claus clinging on to our stubby chimney, wobbling ominously when the wind got up.

It was the metre-high fibreglass snowman in the front flower bed that lurched from side to side and sang "Winter Wonderland" if you got within sneezing distance and set off its sensor.

It was the leafy magnolia tree in the middle of the lawn, covered in baubles and tinsel and fake icicles, and topped with a slightly squint silvery star.

It was the fact that it was mid-July.

"*You've got to come back when it's dark, once the lights are on, for the full effect!*" said Iris, imitating my dad's soft Welsh accent perfectly.

Well done her; she'd practically managed to synch her impersonation with him actually talking. From here, I could see Dad's mouth moving as he explained the point of our out-of-season festive home to the bemused young mum.

Or maybe it wasn't so much the house that was

bemusing her. It was probably just bizarre in general to come across an unseasonably jolly building and then find yourself being talked at by a *clown*, of all people, when all you were trying to do was go out for a nice stroll with your toddler on his push-along trike.

"Iris, have you noticed that the kid's more interested in Dolly?!" I said, as we hoicked up our guitars and headed along the pavement. "He couldn't care less that his mum's having a conversation with a man with a giant red nose!"

Doesn't that just *kill* you about really little kids? They're not too hot on what's real life and what's made up, so a bloke in a clown suit in a suburban British garden is absolutely so-what after the first glimpse, but an elderly dog *sleeping* is completely fascinating.

Still, I suppose the *weird* part was that Dolly was sleeping standing up.

". . .and this is our donations' box," I could now hear Dad saying, pointing a puffy white-gloved hand at the wooden box with the slot on top which was attached to the side of our garden gate.

Beside the gate was a painted sign on a metal stick, which read:

I wish it could be Christmas every day!!
Like our permanent display? Then put a donation in the box. All monies for the Woods Hill Children's Hospital.
Merry Christmas!!

Dolly (stocky, heavy and round) was leaning casually against the metal stick (thin, metal, bending), with her eyes closed, snoring loudly.

It's a talent to be able to do that, it really is. And it's only started since Dolly got doggy dementia.

See – there's always something good to come out of something bad, isn't there?

"Look! Doggy! Look! Doggy! Look! Doggy!" The little kid was badgering his mother, tugging hard at her arm.

"Yes, honey," the mum said vaguely. She was probably making a mental note that 37 Priory Avenue might be some kind of rest home for the criminally insane. Still, at least she gave her kid some coins for the box.

"Ah, here are my girls!" Dad suddenly announced as he spotted me and Iris, his clown smile widening to a giant red banana beam.

The mum spun round expectantly, and looked almost shocked to see two ordinary teenagers in canvas shoes and floppy fringes.

"Your daughters?" she asked Dad.

I think she was relieved to see that we weren't mini-versions of him, with size 40 novelty black boots on, or nylon, grass-green afros perched on top of our heads. (Though she did frown a little when we both swerved around apparently *nothing* on the pavement. It wouldn't have clicked with her that we were automatically veering to the right to avoid the singing snowman's sensor.)

"Near enough," Dad laughed, confusing her just a little bit more.

What he meant was we're like twins, practically (though I'm more reserved, and Iris is a bit dippier). And of course I *am* his daughter (naturally), and Iris is at our house (and I'm at hers) all the time so it's like she's as much a part of the family as Gracie.

As Gracie *was*, I mean.

Or is she *still*?

I'm never exactly sure. . .

"Woof!" the little kid suddenly barked at snoozing Dolly.

"Rufff!" Dolly doggy-muffled back in her sleep, her jumbled daydreams full of fluff, odd socks, cats-once-chased, or maybe half-remembered girls with grey eyes.

"Anyway, time's marching on. Got to get to work!" Dad said brightly to the young mum, as he waved his fat-gloved hand at her child and flip-flapped off towards the front door.

"Um, bye," she answered hesitantly.

"He's an accountant," Iris said matter-of-factly to the mum as we sauntered by, heading through the gate.

I gave such a snort of laughter that my guitar whacked me on the back of the head again.

Iris didn't notice this time – she was too busy following in Dad's oversized footsteps, suddenly reverting to the conversation we'd been having before her knee went squeaky, i.e., moaning about the lousy tunes we always had to do for school orchestra.

Unnoticed, I held back, rubbing my head again. And in that grumpy second, I caught sight of a reflection in the stained glass window by the side of the front door; hazily visible on the pink leaded roses was a face I hadn't seen for a long, long time.

"Gracie?!" I blurted out, spinning around to see her.

But there was no one there – just an empty piece of pavement now that the mum and kid had shuffled away in bamboozlement.

A shiver rippled up and down my spine, from my bumped head down and back again.

"Where *are* you?" I muttered, in a voice quieter than a whisper.

"Whumphf?"

These days, Dolly might not take any notice of a commercial airliner doing an emergency landing in our road, but strangely, she managed to hear what I'd just said.

"Whumphf?" she grumbled again, opening her tiny, watery eyes and padding stiffly over towards me.

"Do you miss her?" I asked softly, bending down to give our old pet a comforting pat.

And yes, thwacked myself on the back of the head at the same time.

You know, I'm not just the daughter of a clown; I *am* a clown. . .

Chapter 2

Spook!

Blam – it hit me.

Not my guitar case this time; just my own sheer *dumb*-ness.

"Stupid, stupid, stupid. . ." I muttered, as I stepped from sunshine to gloom through the front door.

Of *course* I hadn't just glimpsed some spooky, spectral vision of Gracie.

It had been *my* reflection.

I'd seen *my* face gazing back at me wide-eyed from the pink stained glass.

But it was still a shock, spotting that surprisingly familiar-ish flash of Gracie's features in mine, I mean.

I'd never noticed it before.

Was I *really* starting to look like her?

Had Mum and Dad spotted that? Did that bother them? Maybe it comforted them. Or freaked them out, maybe?

If you looked at the last photo of me and Gracie together – and it was right here in the hallway – you couldn't see the resemblance at *all*.

"Do they have different dads, then?" I remember a customer of Mum's café asking once, when I was small and freckly and podgy, and leaning over my colouring book at a corner table.

I'd actually been picking my nose at the time, but found myself looking up sharply when I heard the comment and Mum's puzzled "Er, no!" in response. She was frowning in confusion at frizzy-haired, six-year-old me and at beautiful, bored teenage Gracie, sitting on one of the squashy café sofas sulkily listening to her favourite R&B tracks on her headphones. You could tell Mum was stunned that the cheeky customer couldn't see our obvious similarities. (To be fair, the cheeky customer must have thought Mum was either in deep denial or registered blind.)

Now, wrestling off my lethal guitar and placing it next to Dad's unicycle, I squinted at the framed photo on the hall wall.

It took a second or two for my eyes to adjust to

the indoor shade after coming in from the bright Saturday morning outside, but suddenly there we were – Gracie and me – in all our mismatching glory.

The photo wasn't just a blow-up of some casual, on-holiday, mooching-on-the-beach type snap. For some unknown reason, Mum and Dad had come up with the bright idea of booking me and Gracie a session at a proper studio, with fancy lights and backdrops and a photographer with a line in terrible jokes that were meant to make us both relax and smile.

Well, the jokes worked on *one* of us at least.

Check me out: apple-fat cheeks (I look marginally less like a guinea pig now), big braced smile (can't remember which of the photographer's terrible jokes got me grinning; the one about the horse and the long face, maybe) and a fringe cut so short I seemed cheerfully surprised at all times (my idea of ultimate style back then).

Gracie had been placed slightly behind me, her smile small, fake and pained, her light brown hair long, sleek and glossy, her pale grey eyes boring into the camera lens with a look that screamed "I REALLY, REALLY DON'T WANT TO BE DOING SOMETHING THIS *CHEESY*!!"

Gracie was nearly eighteen at the time, all cheekbones and attitude. (What you *can't* tell from the picture is that she was silently *sniffing* me.)

I was ten, all wrapped up in ways to bug my superior older sister, in revenge for the constant waves of irritation I felt radiating towards me, whether I deserved them or not. (About five seconds after this shot was taken, the photographer had his hands over his ears as Gracie screamed at me for illegally spraying on some of her DKNY perfume.)

"Do I look like her if I do *this*. . .?" I muttered to myself, copying Gracie's pose of simmering resentment, and then focusing on my reflection in the glass of the frame.

Perhaps it was the hair that made us seem alike now – my frizz had mostly gone, thanks to some expensive products and the occasional use of a pair of hair straighteners (Gracie's).

Right then, my nose twitched, and I half-hoped to sniff that long-forgotten perfume . . . but instead it was just the slightly whiffy odour of an elderly dog.

"All right, Dolly?" I said, shivering thoughts of the sights and smells of Gracie from my mind.

I turned and followed my pooch into the living room. It was a distance of about half a metre, but we moved very, *very* slowly, since Dolly is as wide as a sack of potatoes and about as speedy.

"Iris? Are you in here?" I called out, suddenly remembering my best friend and wondering where she was.

Glancing quickly around the room I saw no sign of her. I'd half-expected to see Iris already draped on one of the sofas, taking the weight off her dangerously squeaky knee.

Maybe I was still feeling slightly rattled, but I spun around to leave a little *too* enthusiastically, which made Dolly jump in a creaky sort of way, and the draught I'd created made the nearest ream of snowflake fairy lights flap and tap against the wall.

The fairy lights are the extent of festive decor *inside* our house, by the way. Mum and Dad gave up on the Christmas tree a long time ago, when hoovering pine needles out of the carpet had became a full-time job (mine).

The Christmas cards disappeared during the spring after Gracie had gone, mainly because we had the windows open to let the April breeze wiffle its way in, and of course the cards went fluttering from the shelves and mantelpiece like a bunch of dried-up old leaves left over from autumn.

But enough with mulling over a certain Christmas past; where *was* Iris?

We didn't exactly live in a mansion, with separate wings and orangeries and servants' quarters, so it took about three seconds to follow the sound of her voice and find her in the kitchen.

"So what do you think it could be, Owen?" Iris was asking my dad, who had put on his regular glasses over the clown make-up and silly big nose and was obligingly bending over to examine my best friend's perfectly healthy leg.

He wasn't the *only* clown in the room, by the way.

A skinnier, younger clown in stripy dungarees and a purple afro wig was sitting at the table, furiously clicking at his mobile phone keypad.

"All right, Spike?" I said, waving vaguely in his direction.

"Uh, great! You OK, Jem?" the junior clown mumbled back, his eyes hardly straying from his mobile.

I didn't bother with an answer cause I didn't think he was particularly looking for one. I'd sort of known Spike for years now, without ever really *knowing* him, if you see what I mean. He wasn't so much the strong, silent type as the *geeky*, silent type. All I could be sure of was the fact that a) he was devoted to Dad, b) he made a very good silent sidekick to Dad's main clown act, and c) he'd often be in our kitchen at weekends, patiently waiting for Dad to be ready, playing games on his phone and saying a shy "Uh, you OK, Jem?" if I happened to wander in the room.

Actually, I'd just remembered that when *Gracie* used to wander into the room, he'd clam up completely. Being gorgeous *and* sarcastic made her pretty intimidating to the average teenage geeky assistant clown, I guess.

For a fleeting second, I wondered how old Spike was now. He'd started out as Dad's weekend/holiday helper when he was still at school, and he was a couple of years into his uni course now, so that had to make him roundabout twenty. . .

Same as Gracie was/is/would be, I mulled, with my head in its usual muddle when I thought about my sister.

"Well, I'm no doctor," my dad the clown was saying, frowning at Iris's knee, "but with a squeak like that, I'd guess you might have a *bolt* loose in there. Or perhaps a small mouse."

Iris blinked in confusion for a sec, like she'd

never been wound up by my dad before, then went to laugh – but cuckoo'd instead.

It's all right; she hadn't gone insane.

She just happened to open her mouth at the *exact* second a flutter of wooden birds clattered out of their doors and began tooting the fact that it was twelve o'clock.

Iris turned to me, mouth still open, her eyebrows arched in pleased surprise.

"Spook!" we said in tandem.

We love them – coincidences, I mean, not the nine cuckoos that leap out every hour on the hour from the nine clocks on their various spots on our kitchen wall. (Well, *nearly* every hour – Mum flicks their switches to "off" after tea, so they don't disturb us during important stuff, like watching telly and sleeping. They're allowed to toot and coo again in the morning, their doors slapping open just as the radio DJ does a time-check at seven a.m.)

I can't remember which one of us came up with "Spook!", but for me and Iris, it's our coincidence code word. It's what we rush to blurt out when we've been gossiping about someone and they walk around the corner, or when we both turn up wearing the same colour T-shirt, or when a track comes on the radio that we've only *just* been trying to work out parts for on our guitars.

We're also very into any kind of strangeness, from real-life stories in magazines about ordinary people being reincarnations of Boudicca and Tutankhamen or whoever to corny but eerie ghost-hunting telly programmes. And don't get us started on random bizarreness; only last week, I met Iris in the park after she got her hair cut and she got as far as saying "So, do you like—" when a pigeon pooed on her fringe. Now you can't say that's not spooky, can you?

"Are you getting Suzanne another clock for her birthday *this* year?" Iris turned and asked Dad.

"Certainly am!" Dad nodded, while taking his glasses off and reaching over to grab the handle on the large gold box on the kitchen table. "Found it on eBay – it's a genuine antique!"

"And we're *genuinely* going to run out of space!" I told him, nodding at the kitchen wall, where other people might have something useful like a cupboard or shelves for mugs and pots and pans.

Dad can't resist buying a clock for Mum every time he comes across one. As romantic gestures go, they might seem kind of *screwy* compared to flowers and roses, but it's all cause my parents met

in Switzerland – home of cuckoo clocks – w[illegible]
Mum was waitressing in her uni gap year and where
Dad (aged twenty-two at the time) had landed on
his round-the-world travels, paid for by clowning
and conjuring at festivals and fairs wherever he'd
shipped up.

"I'll just have to magic up an extra wall, then, won't I?" Dad grinned, holding on to the gold box, which was a) part of his magic act and b) now *jiggling*.

Yes, my world is slightly strange. Which is why I like to retreat to a calmer, more sane part of the house whenever I can.

"Coming?" I asked Iris, beckoning her towards the stairs with a tilt of my head.

I fancied lazing the next few hours away in my bedroom, listening to music, flicking through some magazines, and chatting about not-very-much with my best friend.

Except it wasn't going to happen.

"Um, Mr W?" I heard Spike say warily, as I made to grab a couple of cartons of juice from the fridge.

Shutting the fridge door, I saw Dad lean over – wobbly gold box in hand – and peer at the screen of the phone that Spike was holding up for him to read.

not in a good way.

orried, as if he was expecting a face any second.

I should have followed a limping Iris itchen there and then. Or I should have se anger and made up an on-the-spot reason why I needed to leave the house instantly, if not sooner.

I definitely *shouldn't* have said the following two very innocent-sounding words. . .

"What's up?"

But then I can always be relied on to say stuff I'll regret, can't I?

"Jem . . . there's been a bit of a hiccup," Dad muttered, with an apologetic shrug. "And I might just need your help. Urgently."

As if it was sensing how urgent the situation was, the gold box – which contained a large white rabbit called Arnold – began to wibble more violently.

It was then that I noticed that Spike had turned his worried gaze from my dad to me. It was very *eerie* having two clowns staring at you so intensely.

And then it clicked.

"Oh no!! Not *that*!" I groaned, suddenly realizing I was in big, BIG trouble. . .

Chapter 3

Shoot me now, why don't you?

Yummy Fun.

It's exactly what I *wasn't* going to have this afternoon.

I stepped under the sign – with the "Y" and the "F" painted to look like huge squashy marshmallows – and into the crowded café in the park.

There was Mum behind the counter in her uniform of T-shirt, jeans and pink embroidered apron, with her hair pinned up in a muddle of dark curls and a smile like sunshine. She even had a rainbow above her head – though that had more to do with the poster on the wall behind her advertising a summer concert in the park than anything to do with her personality.

"Oh, dear. . ." said Mum, her smile fading as she caught sight of me weaving between the bouncing toddlers towards her.

I quickly whipped off the purple nylon afro, assuming she was oh dear-ing because the kids were now paying *me* more attention than Jeff, the guy who she got to come and do a Sing-Along-A-Nursery-Rhyme session in the café three times a week.

"I guess this means Spike got that job?" Mum asked as I arrived at the cake-filled counter, swerving to avoid a crawling baby or two.

Spike Hawkins – he was quite possibly my least favourite person in the universe right at that moment.

"Not for sure," I shrugged, bending down to turn up one uncomfortably unravelling long leg of the stripy dungarees I was wearing and coming eye-to-eye with a small baby face covered in lunch gloop and green snot. It wasn't a pretty sight. I straightened up quickly. "Someone in the computer store is off sick, so they asked him to come in to cover the shift, as a sort of test to see if he likes the job, and if they like him."

"Oh, dear. . ." Mum murmured again, shaking her head thoughtfully and making the tumble of curls bobble about. "Still, unless Spike really messes up, I guess your dad will have to find himself a new weekend helper!"

Well, yeah! I thought wearily, wondering if Dad

would now stop burying his head in the sand and accept that Spike was going to hand in his notice. I mean, Spike might have been an excellent magician's assistant/deputy clown for the past five years, but considering he was now doing a degree in computing, it was no big wow that he was trying to get a part-time job that had more to do with computers than balloon animals.

Of course, my dad didn't get it. I mean, how could talking customers through the latest Mac operating system compare to the fun of making a multicoloured twit of yourself in front of thirty squealing five-year-olds?

That head-burying thing; it's why Dad smiled but carried on regardless when Spike warned him *months* ago that he'd be applying for other jobs. It's why he'd been so surprised and unprepared when Spike got an interview with the computer store in the shopping centre last month. (And why I got roped in that time to help at some kid's party Dad was booked to perform at. How had I managed to get roped in *again*?!)

"Anyway, can I have it?" I asked Mum, suddenly remembering what I'd come for. "Dad'll be wondering where I've gone."

"Oh, of course," said Mum, all of a fluster, hurrying over to a tall cupboard that was painted with gambolling rabbits and deer.

She wrestled something out and – with difficulty – handed it to me.

"You haven't got a bag, have you?" I asked hopefully.

Naturally, Mum didn't have a bag big enough for it, and *naturally*, I had to walk the walk of shame from the café through the park to Dad's van while tripping over a life-size fluffy ostrich. . .

Dolly – sitting bolt upright between us – was happily yodelling along to some old song on the radio (Dad swore she preferred Radio 2).

Arnold – our pet rabbit – was sitting in my lap, nibbling at my nose (the plastic red one I was holding in my hand).

I hate leaving Arnold inside her gold box. She has to stay in it for ages at parties, cause her starring role always comes at the end of Dad's act.

"You know, it took me *ages* to think where I'd left it," said Dad brightly, as we pootled through the early afternoon traffic.

Um, how do you forget a giant bird costume? You'd

think Dad would have a pretty clear memory of last Sunday, when there was a little girl's birthday party in Mum's café and Dad was on entertaining duty. Me and Iris watched from the safety of one of the tables outside, as he lolloped about like he was riding the ostrich, with his lower body *inside* the costume and its yellow legs (fake, padded "human" legs dangled by its sides), while his upper body was his standard clown self, holding on to a pair of reins.

A normal person would pretty much recall that straightaway, you'd suppose. But for Dad, being half-man, half-ostrich was as mundane as filing a report.

"So . . . one more week of school, eh, Jem?" Dad said now, very cheerfully.

I didn't say anything back. Not cause I was being rude, but because I immediately panicked that if school summer holidays = Dad's busiest time, and Spike getting a new job = Dad being short of an assistant, then that might equal a whole lot of unwanted work for me. I might need to do something drastic, like vanish, same as Gracie did.

(OK, bad joke, I know. *Really* bad joke, actually. Sorry.)

"Hey, do you really need those, Jem?" Dad asked, changing tack as he glanced sideways at me.

It's pretty rich of a guy in full clown make-up to question the fact that I was wearing a pair of sunglasses on a not-too-sunny day.

"Yes, I absolutely do," I answered firmly, as I shrank further down in the passenger seat with Arnold.

The way I reckoned it was this: *yes*, I was sitting in a van painted lurid colours with *Mr Wiggle's World of Giggles* splashed all over it, and *yes*, I was wearing a pair of stripy dungarees, but if I kept the purple afro wig and face paint in the bag at my feet till the last minute, then *maybe* I could end up looking like the only normal creature in the van if anyone passing by happened to stare at us.

To prove my point, we ground to a halt at a red light, and straightaway a couple of lads in baseball caps slowed down as they hip-hopped their way along the pavement nearest to me, and began pointing and jeering at either Dad, Dad's van, or yodelling Dolly.

I surreptitiously reached over to the button that would make the van window go up.

I pressed hard.

The window didn't budge (great).

I slunk lower.

It's not me they're looking at, I reminded myself.

"Oi, darlin'!!" one of the lads blurted, as he lunged towards my open window. "Goin' to give's a wiggle, then?"

For a millisecond I had no idea what he meant, till I remembered the logo on the side of the van, in giant, technicolour letters. Sigh. . .

"Go on, you know you want to!" he continued in a stupid, mocking voice while his mate cackled in the background.

OK. In certain circumstances I'm as embarrassed as Gracie used to be by Dad's dumb job, but on the other hand, it's pretty great to be the daughter of a guy who does something non-normal and non-dull. These baseball-cap boys would *always* be dull. Not to mention obnoxious and stupid.

"Get lost!" I barked at the moron nearest to me, my sudden courage coming out of nowhere. "Or I'll set my rabbit on you!"

I held up a white-furred, floppy-eared Arnold and squeezed. Some strange reflex happens when you do that, and Arnold bared a mean set of sharp teeth.

"All right! All right! Keep your hair on!!" snorted moron-boy, while Moron No. Two hooted with laughter and pointed at my head.

Ahhh . . . so the purple afro *wasn't* in the bag.

It was on my head, where I'd stuck it when I was struggling to carry the ostrich through the park.

"*DOOP-DOODLY-OOP-DOOP, DOOP-DOOP!*" blasted Dad's deafening cartoon-tune van horn, making the hip-hopping lads jump out of their too-cool skins.

"Bye, boys!" Dad yelled, simultaneously moving on as the traffic lights changed and taking his hand off the horn. "Where's a cream pie when you need one, eh, Jem?"

I bent around Dolly to see Dad better. "Doesn't it ever bother you? Coming across idiots like that?"

What a dumb question.

It's obvious that Dad *loves* his job, and gets a huge kick out of the fact that just showing up in his stupid clown costume cheers people up before he even *starts* on his magic acts or balloon wombats or falling-over gags or whatever.

"Jem, honey, not all lads are like *those* lads," Dad replied amiably, as we headed on along the high street, with Saturday shoppers stopping in their tracks and smiling at the sight of the van, Mr Wiggle and me. . .

*

And how right Dad was.

As if by magic – spook! – I was currently under a table with a very non-obnoxious boy indeed.

"Ooof!" he sighed, as he made a useless grab for Arnold and missed.

With a flick of her bobbed tail, Arnold hopped out from under the draped *Toy Story* tablecloth. She vanished – at her own risk – into the whirling throng of small, overexcited, over-sugared six-year-olds stomping around to Michael Jackson's *Thriller* while they waited for their parents to come and pick them up.

But even though I needed to find Arnold fast-ish, I suddenly found myself in no hurry to get out of this hidden-away oasis of calm. Maybe it was cause I needed a quick breather, after putting up with an hour of shrieking, squealing, honking, roaring and madness.

Or maybe it was more to do with who I was under the table *with*. . .

"Hey, your rabbit – he's *fast*!" laughed the boy, sprawled beside me on his stomach.

"Arnold's a *she*, actually," I told him, shoving my dopey purple afro back so I could see the boy better. On second thought, I yanked it off completely and ruffled my hair, so he could spot I was girl about his age and not just some random, idiot work experience clown who'd managed to lose the starring act in Mr Wiggle's show.

"A *she*? How come?" my under-table companion asked. This close up, his hair was very dark and his eyes were velvety brown to match.

"Dad's had loads of rabbits over the years, and they're always called Arnold. It's a tradition, I s'pose. Well, actually, it's also because the name 'Arnold' is painted on the side of his van too, beside a picture of a big, white rabbit. . ."

I finished my sentence with a *there-you-go* shrug.

The boy smiled an *I-get-it!* smile back.

Of course, he didn't know it, but *he* was the reason I'd managed to lose Arnold in the first place, accidentally letting her jump out of my arms, in between Dad magicking her out of a bashed bowler hat and me supposedly fastening her safely back into her gold box.

It's just that it's *extremely* hard to concentrate on silliness when you're faced with someone very cute while you're dressed like a buffoon and dying of embarrassment.

And apart from losing Arnold while Dad was

taking his bow (and squirting water at everyone in the audience) the boy was *also* the reason I'd dropped the soft toy kittens Dad passed to me after his juggling trick; messed up the bit when I was meant to catch the flowers Dad was "pulling" out of some kid's ears; and forgot to run around pretending to be scared when Dad dressed up in his ostrich costume (I'd had my mobile on the table behind Arnold's box and been surreptitiously texting Iris about the birthday boy's cute big brother).

"So you're *Miss* Wiggle, then?" the boy asked me with a grin, leaning his chin on his hand.

"Miss Wisniewski, actually," I told him, since – surprise, surprise – Wiggle is not on my birth certificate.

"Wizz— Whizz—?" he stumbled.

"You say it like 'Wish–nef–ski'," I explained, like I always had to. "It's Polish. From way back. A great-grandfather I never met."

I could see that the boy was wearing the sort of puzzled expression people have when they stop outside our house and gawp at the decorations. I appreciated that it was probably just as hard for him to get his head around the fact that he was under a table with the daughter of a Welsh-sounding Polish clown.

But ha – *nothing* about our family was ever straightforward.

"Right. . . Uh, by the way, did you know that your face paint's smudged?" said the boy, frowning at me, then – eek! – reaching out to rub at a spot to the left of my mouth. "Oops . . . sorry, I think I made it worse!"

"No worries. Looking stupid's what clowns do best!" I replied brightly.

I felt quite proud of myself, under the circumstances. I'd come up with a breezy line, even though I was under a table with a cute boy, ridiculous clown make-up smudged across my face, and a tummy full of fluster.

Mind you, it was freaking me out how much he was staring at me right now. . .

"Hey, *I* know who you are!" he suddenly blurted out. "You're that girl whose sister disappeared! I remember your name . . . and your family being in the paper!"

My cute-boy fluster instantly evaporated, replaced with a wave of stress and irritation.

"It's not a *magic* trick!" I blustered, suddenly tapping into that faint flash of temper I'd had at the traffic lights earlier. "Gracie didn't 'vanish'! She just *chose* to go!"

I tried to scramble out from under the table

with as much dignity as too-long trouser legs and a handful of afro curls would allow and stormed off in search of Arnold.

The thing is, no one outside of the family ever talks about Gracie now. I guess they all started to realize they could only ask "Any news of Gracie?" so many times before it made Mum upset or they felt horrendously awkward, so they stopped.

And I like it that way.

I'm OK with mentions of Gracie that are nothing-y and ordinary. It's fine if Iris points out a dress in the window of TopShop that looks a lot like one Gracie used to have, or if Dad remembers out loud that Gracie had played the part of Tallulah in the school's production of *Bugsy Malone* when I tell him I'm in the orchestra for *this* year's production.

All that day-to-day stuff is cool. It's just the dramatic stuff I don't much like.

Which is why I've got this box in my head. One that is *not* gold and definitely *doesn't* have a rabbit in it. . .

My form teacher Mrs McLennan brought up the subject of the box during a casual chat we had that turned out to be not-so-casual.

"Fancy popping in to see me at break time, Jem?"

she asked, about a month after Gracie had gone.

I knew what was up; I was moping around, doing no homework. So she gave me the sympathy talk; said I could come to her any time I wanted, and suggested the box.

"It's important to talk about your sister as much as you want to, Jem," she'd said, passing me my third tissue, "but sometimes it helps just to step away from all the heavy feelings and be normal."

Wow, how I'd *loved* the idea of feeling normal at that time.

"Here's what I think: try to imagine a box in your head."

Excuse me?! I'd felt like blurting out.

"Try and visualize putting all your hurt and worry and anger in there and locking it up. It's not that you're ignoring your memories and feelings; it's just that you're giving yourself a break from it."

Oh, a break . . . yes, please! my frazzled brain sighed.

"And you can open up the box and look inside whenever you like."

Nice idea. I even pictured it being blue, to match my mood whenever I thought about Gracie. Trouble was, I didn't ever like to open the stupid thing.

And I hadn't ever told anyone – not Mum, not Dad, not even Iris – that except for today, I've thought of Gracie a little bit less (OK, quite a *lot* less) as time has trailed by. Can I help it if my life is busy, and secondary school has been great? Does that make me a really horrible person?

A really horrible *sister*?

"Arnold!!" I called out, snapping the lid of the box firmly closed in my head and scanning the messed-up party room for signs of a bunny on the loose, or any kid trying to stuff a reluctant rabbit into their party bag.

Ah . . . bingo!

"Hey, thanks very much for finding my rabbit!" I said, suddenly swooping on a kid sitting at the end of the long table.

The kid – the birthday boy, I realized – was stroking Arnold in his lap and trying to feed her a leftover half-a-sausage from the dregs of the buffet. "I've been looking *everywhere* for . . . um. . ."

My little speech was cut short, as my eyes spied a handwritten name-place card strewn in the general carnage of the table.

Gracie, it said.

Spook! I thought.

I lifted Arnold from the boy – blocking out his roar of protest – and tried to think myself sensible. Yes, it was a coincidence that one second I'm under a table (not wanting to be) talking about her, and the next I'm staring at my sister's name scrawled in gold pen.

Yeah, but it's a pretty common name nowadays, I reminded myself, as I wiped a splodge of tomato sauce off Arnold's nose and walked away from the continuing roar.

"Awww! Is the bunny hurt? Is it bleeding?!?" squealed a little girl, skipping up to me in a beautiful peach net dress with chocolate fingerprints all over it and a chocolate mouth to match.

"No – it's just been eating a sausage," I explained, stopping to let her stroke chocolate smears over Arnold's snow-white coat. (I didn't want someone *else* to start roaring.)

"It's *sooooo* cute!" gurgled the little girl. "Can I hold—"

"Gracie! GRACIE!!" came a sudden shout, and the girl spun her head around. "Come on – your mummy's waiting! She's double-parked and blocking Mr Wiggle's van in!"

As *this* Gracie beamed a brown smile at me and

hurried off to collect her party bag, my head raced.

Three mentions of Gracie's name in the space of a minute? I *had* to tell Iris . . . it was more than a spook – it was a super-spook!

"Uh, sorry – I didn't mean to upset you or – or freak you out just then," a voice muttered by my side.

I turned to see the boy shrugging shyly.

My head was so rattled that I couldn't think of anything sensible to say, so I gave him a lopsided smile that I hoped showed I forgave him. Though with my smudged make-up, it probably looked like the demonic grin of a killer zombie clown out of a horror movie.

Phew. He smiled back.

"By the way, my name's – OWWW!!"

Shoot me now, why don't you.

Or maybe my stupid rabbit, which seemed to have mistaken OWWW's finger for another sausage.

"Bye, children!! Bye! Mr Wiggle has got to go!!" Dad's voice cut through the music and mayhem.

Hurray – it was time to do my *own* disappearing act, before my flushed cheeks radiated through my layer of face paint. . .

Chapter 4

The odd house out

Gracie.

Gracie.

Gracie.

Three mentions of her name at the party this afternoon, heaped on top of the swirl of thoughts about her this morning.

"That's a *lot* of Gracies." Iris nodded thoughtfully as she leant forward and examined the side of her pretty much perfect nose in the vast, low-lit mirror above the dual black marble sinks. "Hey, Jem – do you think I should get the doctor to check this out?!"

Yep, that sounded like typical Iris, convincing herself that a standard-issue spot was a type of rare tropical fungal skin disease or whatever. Mind you, she once got our maths teacher seriously in a panic; Iris slapped her hands over her face and started screaming about being in pain. Ms Newton thought Iris was having a seizure or an aneurysm or something. Actually, Iris had just applied mint lipgloss, then went and rubbed her eye with the same finger. . .

"Nope – it's a zit," I told her bluntly. "Anyway, the whole Gracie thing has been wall-to-wall *weird*."

It was Saturday evening and me, Mum and Dad were at Iris's house for tea. And while my parents and Iris's were yakking at the dining room table, me and Iris had nipped up to the loo, which – in Iris's house at least – is a very unnerving place to be. It's cause of the door. Call me fussy, but I like the idea of bathroom doors that you can *lock*. The Fletchers' loo might look like something out of a spa, but for safety's sake, you've got to go in pairs. . .

"I've probably just got Gracie on the brain, cause of it being our mum's birthday tomorrow," I suggested, reaching out for some loo roll.

Only there was nothing on the wall except two plaster-crumbly holes.

"Oh, yeah . . . don't worry about that – the holder fell off this morning," Iris explained airily. "Anyway, just cause you've been thinking about Gracie, it doesn't explain why a total stranger suddenly starts talking about her under a table, or a kid with the same name suddenly pops up in front of you, on paper *and* in person!"

While Iris contemplated the coincidence (as well as her non-existent spot), I bent down and made a grab for the scented loo roll that was unravelling over the expensively tiled floor.

Yep, that summed up Iris's fabulous yet wonky home.

She only lives across the road and up a bit, but hers is *definitely* the odd house out. Where *my* 1930s terraced house matches the rest of the street, *Iris's* is an architect-designed glass and concrete box, built about six years ago in the space next to No. 18, where a scrappy patch of wasteland used to be.

Mine is packed with Christmas lights, cuckoo clocks and clown paraphernalia; hers is all streamlined and minimal, like something out of a glossy interiors mag. *My* house is gadget-free (unless you count the timer on the cooker), while hers is a gizmo-nerd's paradise (the Fletchers have one remote that controls the temperature, the blinds and the ambient music that can be piped into every room).

But here's an interesting point: in my bizarrely

decorated, knick-knack-centric lo-fi home, *everything* works like the manual says it will. In Iris's state-of-the-art home, most things don't. Work, that is. Unless of course the original architect *meant* for the temperature to waver excitingly from Mediterranean to Arctic, the blinds to stay stuck at an intriguing halfway open/halfway shut point, and illegal ragga radio stations to cut into the ambient music when you least expect it.

Still, it would been nice if just the lock on the *loo* worked, if nothing else.

The thick bathroom door has some fancy, space age, microchipped mechanism inside it that jams if you ever try to lock it and traps you inside (not my dream way to spend an evening). It's a case of keeping your fingers crossed that no one will walk in on you with your knickers round your knees. . .

"Oh! Oops! Sorry, Jem!!"

Great.

The person barging in right now was Viv, Iris's mum. She immediately slapped her hand over her eyes.

"*Knock*, Mum, remember?!" Iris spun round and reprimanded her with a roll of her eyes.

"Silly me!" Viv laughed, backing out of the room

in a flap of her bejewelled flip-flops.

"It's fine! I'm done!" I said quickly, standing up and smoothing down the cotton of my shorty smock dress while breathing a sigh of relief that Iris's mum hadn't walked in half a second earlier.

The daisy-covered smock: I'd traded that in for this afternoon's stripy dungarees, and switched the purple afro for bow-shaped clips in my hair. I didn't usually get so dressed up just to hang out at Iris's, but this evening her mum Viv and dad Ray had invited my family round for tea, in honour of Mum's birthday. OK, so they were celebrating a day early, but Mum preferred her actual birthday to be as low-key and fuss-free as possible.

At least she had since . . . well, you *know* what since.

Back in the box, I told myself quickly.

With a swift check in the mammoth mirrors (good, no stray smears of clown make-up behind my ears), I turned to leave – and found my head unexpectedly cupped in a pair of hands.

"Let me look at you, Jemima, sweetheart. . ." Viv said warmly, gazing earnestly into my face.

Eek – I'm not very good at earnestness. It reminds me too much of all the sympathetic head-tilting that went on a couple of years ago. Back then, it was as if there was an epidemic of cricked necks amongst every adult friend, neighbour, shopkeeper and schoolteacher I knew.

"*You*, my sweetheart, are getting to be *so* like your sister," said Viv, squeezing my cheeks between her palms.

Wow, I'd no idea Gracie looked so much like a chipmunk.

"Mum – how much wine have you had?" I heard Iris ask, from somewhere to my left.

Hurray for my best friend and her mum-teasing; she *knew* I'd be squirming.

"Shush, Iris!" murmured Viv, never moving her eyes from my squished face. It must have been like staring at an overfed pufferfish. "Your poor mum, Jem . . . watching you grow more and *more* like Gracie. . ."

I hoped not. I liked to think I was pleasant, sociable and friendly, i.e., the exact opposite of my big sister.

But seriously, Mum didn't *really* think that, I was sure. It was just lovely Viv getting sad and sentimental over a glass of wine (or three).

"*Mum*," Iris said in a gentle "maybe-that's-enough" warning tone, as used by mums in the

Yummy Fun café when their kids start whacking Jeff the entertainer on the legs with their Jelly Cats and Bionicles while he's trying to do a verse of "The Wheels On The Bus".

Viv ignored her.

"You know, Jem, Suzanne misses your sister *every* day, but it must be *so* much worse when it's her birthday. She must *so* hope she hears from her at a time like this!!"

Before I got a chance to ponder on that, and wonder if it was true, the face-cupping had been replaced by a bear hug (if you can imagine a bear in Monsoon linen shift dress with a very nice French manicure).

Ouch.

That hurt.

The pang of guilt, I mean.

I get that sometimes, when there's a mention of Gracie.

It isn't just the unspoken guilt of not missing her often enough. It's a deep-down guilt that I can't quite weasel out of some distant, dusty corner of my mind.

And it's more than the guilt too; there's all this *other* stuff that starts slithering out of the box marked *Gracie* in my head. Stuff I don't really want to think too much about, like embarrassment, anger, confusion, numbness. . .

It's very, *very* complicated, having a sister who's not there, that's all I can say.

"Poor Jem," Viv muttered into my hair, her red lips giving me a peck on the, er, hair clip, one manicured hand rubbing my back.

In the movies, this tender moment would come complete with soaring violins. An audience's tears would be jerked, their heart-strings pulled.

But in a sudden rush of panic, I realized with deep shame that there was something I *hadn't* pulled.

Trying not to disturb Viv's well-meant bear hug, I stretched one arm out – and flushed the loo.

Hey, welcome to my non-glossy world. . .

Chapter 5

A something or a nothing?

The music was faint.

So faint, it was a bit like listening to an old-fashioned merry-go-round ride, down a phone you were holding away from your head.

So faint, I'd have thought I was dreaming it, if I wasn't sitting upright on the edge of my bed, straining my ears.

1.35 a.m., the time flashed luminously on my bedside clock. I hadn't felt like I could sleep when I first lay wide-eyed under my squashy duvet. But somehow I'd nodded off, and Saturday night had quietly slithered into the dark hours of Sunday morning.

So what was with the faint, faraway music? Had Mum or Dad left the telly on downstairs? Could one of them have fallen asleep in front of it, or gone to lock up and wandered upstairs, oblivious to some late night/early hours programme noodling away unwatched on the TV?

But it wouldn't be like *either* of them to do that. One might be a clown and the other one ditzy, but Mum and Dad were both pretty (surprisingly) organized when it came to mundane stuff like paying for school dinners and having enough milk and switching off tellies at night.

Though maybe they're allowed one *night off being grown-up and sensible*, I told myself, slipping my bare feet down on to the soft rag rug on my bedroom floor. *A couple of glasses of birthday champagne muddled up with thoughts of you-know-who, and it'd be no big surprise if they forgot the mundane stuff for once. . .*

I pulled open my bedroom door – and stopped in nerve-jangling shock.

In the gloom of the hall, my eyes had focused on a low, black mound hunched on the polished floorboards.

A slightly *vibrating* black mound.

And it seemed to be *scratching* at Gracie's closed bedroom door opposite.

Scratching . . . and softly *yodelling*.

"Dolly!" I whispered in relief, dropping to my knees by my geriatric dog's side. "Was it *you* I heard?!"

A doggy yodel didn't sound much like faraway fairground jangly music, but then again, my brain was probably semi-furred-up with sleep and dreams.

I wrapped an arm around Dolly's trembling, smooth-furred girth, doing my best to soothe her.

Since her doggy dementia set in, she didn't come to Gracie's door any more. It was as if she'd forgotten not only Gracie but the fact that there had ever been a room along this corridor that she'd once been very happy to slump in. Her tiny English Bull Terrier eyes – all cataracted – didn't even seem to register that there was a *door* in the wall whenever she thumpered along this way.

Till now, that is.

"Hey . . . did *you* hear something too?" I murmured, feeling her weight fall against me, my comforting arm doing the trick.

Then I felt that fleeting prickle of jangling nerves again: had Dolly heard *her* something coming from in *there*?!

I stayed still, listening.

There was nothing now; no tinkly fairground music, however faint.

Nothing except for a repetitive doggy pant.

For another minute I sat still as a statue, ears as cocked and attuned as a dog's (without dementia).

Lots more nothing.

But here we were – Dolly and me – and here was Gracie's door. Inside was a world neither of us entered any more. Though it wasn't exactly what you might call a "secret" world. Not when Mum flung the door open once a week to scoop the unslept-in sheet and duvet cover from the bed, so she could throw it into the mound of family laundry. The door would be open again a day later, as a freshly scented sheet and duvet cover was duly wrangled and flapped and tucked into place, just in case anyone should want to come and cosy down there that night. (No one had, in, like . . . 940 days. Not that I was counting. Though I knew *Mum* was – all you had to do was check out the tally at the end of every month on the "Cornish Scenes" calendar on the kitchen wall.)

Whether me and/or Dolly had heard a something or a nothing, my hand seemed to be on a mission – it was already reaching for the door handle.

"Come on," I said to the mound that was Dolly.

"Hurrumph!!" whumphed Dolly, waking up from her nano-sleep against my knee.

Together, we padded (and waddled) in.

I shut the door softly behind us, at the same time reaching automatically for the light switch.

Flick!

Nothing happened.

Of course: Gracie didn't like bright, overhead lights. She took out the bulb, so she – or anyone else – could never have the choice to switch it on anyway. And that was Gracie all over: no one else's opinions mattered except Gracie's, no one else's convenience. It didn't bother Gracie that Mum might want to switch on the bright light on a dull winter's day when she came in to hoover or change the bedding.

While I fidgeted uselessly with the fiddly switch of the bedside lamp, Dolly waddled around in the dark, occasionally stopping to sniff or bump into things.

Ping!

A soft peachy glow illuminated a comfortingly unfamiliar room.

I mean, yeah, of *course* I'd peeked in here plenty of times over the years, but I seriously never got a toe beyond the brass carpet tread of the doorway before I was yelled at to "GET OUT, JEM!!"

And even though there was no one around to yell

that any more, I think I'd stuck to Gracie's rigid rules like a well-trained dog; one that could be trusted to be left in a room full of sausages yet wouldn't touch a single one till his owner gave him the nod. I hadn't sneaked a look, I hadn't scavenged a thing. If you want proof, the only reason I had Gracie's hair straighteners were because she'd always kept them plugged in on the landing, beside the long mirror, so that felt like a legitimate "borrow" to me.

But suddenly, I felt in the mood to be the dog that finally ate the sausages. Cause I'd just broken Rule No. 1 ("DO <u>NOT</u> COME INTO MY ROOM!!"), and was currently about to break Rule No. 2 ("DO <u>NOT</u> TOUCH MY STUFF").

Wandering around, I let my fingers skim over necklaces I was never allowed to wear, make-up I was never allowed to try and books and mags that I was never allowed to read.

I stopped when I came to Gracie's musical jewellery box, the one she got from Granny, I think. Slowly, I traced the corny painted butterflies that decorated it with my finger.

At the same time, *inside* my head, a spotlight lit up *another* box, where a lid was lifting, letting a certain memory spill out. . .

One day before the wish

"What are you doing?" I ask her, hovering at the doorway.

I've been finding it hard to concentrate on my guitar practice with all the thudding and banging going on.

"I'm building a life-size statue of Queen Victoria made entirely from cornflakes – what does it *look* like?" Gracie drones, not looking up at me as she drops what look like old scrapbooks into a cardboard box.

Other boxes and black plastic bins are already piled and straining with random whatevers from the clear-out my sister is obviously having.

"Yeah, but *that's* your nursery yearbook!" I gasp, recognizing the bits of crêpe paper and pipe cleaners that are sticking out of it. Mine is under my bed, in a pull-out drawer packed with broken Polly Pockets and assorted Peppa Pig jigsaws that I can't bear to dump, even though I'm eleven. "You can't chuck *that*!"

"Jem, I can chuck what I *want*," Gracie snaps in her

best bored voice, lifting her grey eyes to stare straight at me.

From the bits I can see, it seems like she's getting rid of everything that reminds her of being a kid. Mind you, that's nothing new; she's always been breathtakingly unsentimental. A year after our auntie's wedding I *still* sigh when I look at the beautiful satin flower-girl shoes that don't fit me any more, and remember how I cried when I realized the freesias I'd tried to press from my bouquet had turned to dust. But a *week* after our auntie's wedding and Mum caught Gracie stuffing her bridesmaid's dress into a Cancer Research charity bag that had come through the door. "Well, I'm never going to wear it again, am I?" she'd said matter-of-factly.

"Mum won't like it. . ." I mumble from the doorway now, as I picture the living room shelves downstairs, crammed not just with photos of me and Gracie at all ages and stages, but with every single glitter-speckled Mother's Day card we've ever made her, every terrible handmade pottery blob we've presented her with . . . there are even tiny glass boxes with our baby teeth inside, wrapped up lovingly in pink cotton wool.

"In *case* you hadn't noticed, Jem, I'm eighteen now," says Gracie, reaching over to an overflowing black plastic bin bag and forcing a foot inside to stomp flat whatever old treasures lurk in there. "I can do what I *like*."

I have a funny feeling that she would like to be doing that stomping to my *head*. It might be very, very tiring for Gracie to have a dull kid sister always floating around like the pong of a blocked drain, but it's also very, very tiring being permanently despised by a close member of your family.

"You can't do what you like *all* the time," I mumble rebelliously.

I just remembered what Mum told me this morning, while I was hanging out with her down at the café. I'd been doing my homework, and was only half paying attention. But now what she said mattered a *lot* – especially since it's going to deeply annoy my sister.

"What do you mean?" Gracie growls at me. With her long, soft hair, she really is beautiful. Or she would be if she stopped growling for five seconds.

"You have to look after me tomorrow afternoon," I tell her. "Mum says."

"No *way*! I'm going to my friends' drumming show at The Den! Mum knows that! You can just hang out at the café like you normally do, or go round to Iris's. . ."

"Can't," I say back, feeling a bit smug, enjoying torturing her with info she doesn't have. "Mum's got a last-minute appointment with her accountant, Dad's doing a whole bunch of parties and Iris is going out Christmas shopping with her nana. So you *have* to look after me."

Gracie's face is on the edge of fury. She is *so* into those freaky new friends of hers, there's no *way* she'll want to drag me along to anything she's doing with them. I bet she'd rather stuff me in a black plastic bin liner and drag me to the dump, and take her chances on how cross that would make Mum and Dad.

OK, I think it's time to retreat – with one more dig in the form of a sweet smile.

Oh, and maybe I could go back to my guitar practice and strum my way through "Yellow Submarine" by the Beatles. I'm learning that at school, and I know Gracie *really* hates it.

"Aargh!!" I hear her roar, as a missile in the shape of a well-worn Eeyore flies over my head. . .

Chapter 6

Six little words

"The pancakes were gorgeous, Jem!" Mum lied, slipping on her jacket at the door. "We'll have you working in the café kitchen yet!"

Fact: I am a lousy cook. The truth is, my parents have as much chance of me taking over the family firm – whether it's the Yummy Fun café or Mr Wiggle's World of Giggles – as Dolly has of passing an IQ test.

(Dolly made me jump out of my skin when I heard her growling in Gracie's room last night. Till I turned and saw she was staring down her own reflection in the mirror. Don't know what she'd have done if I'd said "Go get it!" Probably headbutted herself.)

"No worries, Mum," I replied, glancing at the brand new diamanté hair combs holding her pile of curls up today. At least I was better at buying sparkly birthday presents than making birthday breakfasts.

"Have a lovely day, Suze," said Dad, leaning past me to kiss Mum. "I've just got that stilt-walking magic show to do at the opening of the new carpet showroom this afternoon, so I'll come pick you up from the café at closing time."

Dad was in disguise, dressed as Owen Wisniewski, in a grey T-shirt, sweatpants, bare feet and bare faced, i.e., his morning Normal Person uniform. Except for the large drill he had in his hand.

"What's that for?" I asked, backing away.

"Just working on a new trick with Arnold!" Dad grinned manically and pressed the on switch so that the drill whirred and whined.

I blinked in horror, momentarily worrying for poor Arnold, when I realized I'd been had. (Wow, I was nearly as gullible as Iris. . .)

"Ignore him," said Mum, lightly kissing me on the forehead. "He's going to put my new cuckoo clock up on the wall, aren't you, Owen?"

"Aw, I was enjoying terrifying my daughter. You spoil all my fun, Suzanne!" Dad joked, switching the drill off and doing doorman duties for Mum instead. "Oh!"

As he yanked open the door, it was Dad's turn to be surprised.

"Eek!" squeaked Iris, sounding pretty surprised herself.

What was she doing, squatting down there on the path?

"Uh, hi, Suzanne!" she said to my mum, as she straightened up quickly, without a single squeak of the knee. "I forgot to give you *this* last night. . ."

Iris was holding a little shiny gift bag that I knew contained novelty flowery rubber gloves. She'd bought them for Mum to use at the café.

". . .but look – I just noticed *this*!"

We all glanced down at the doorstep. It was a simple box of chocolates, no gift wrap – just a pink rosette and what looked like a star-shaped gift tag.

Mum – being the birthday girl – bent to pick it up, a puzzled and expectant small smile on her face.

The morning sun was sending blinding twinkles of light from the strands of glass fairy lights fixed to the fence, so I had to squint as I watched Mum flip the gift tag over and read the message.

"Owen! OWEN!!" she gasped, holding her throat as if it had started to swell, poisoned by my inedible breakfast pancakes.

She thrust the chocolates at my dad, who in alarm tried to grab at them with the hand holding the drill.

"Oops! Ah – got it. What is. . .?"

He clearly didn't know what to look at first: Mum running down the garden path, or the message on the gift tag.

But Iris – followed by a stiffly trotting Dolly – went after Mum.

Which left Dad and me to scan the message that seemed to have shaken my mother so much.

And here's what it said: *Happy Birthday, Mum. With loveness, Gracie xxx*

Wow.

"Suzanne!" Dad called out, hurrying down the path now too.

Mum was on the pavement, staring this way and that up and down the street.

"She was here!" Mum gasped. "When was she here?! She could be just along the road somewhere!"

Mum looked practically demented with hope, some curls tumbling loose, as she swithered from left to right. She seemed poised to run, but unsure which way to take off, in case it was the *wrong* way.

"But probably not," Iris blurted out, bizarrely.

"Wha – what?" Mum asked, still glancing frantically along the length of the deserted Sunday morning road.

"The message!" said Iris, not really answering the question terribly well. She looked completely thrown by Mum's reaction.

I suddenly understood, doing that best friend trick of tuning into Iris's train of thought.

"It's a *printed* message!" I said to Dad, as I took the box from his hands and hurried over with it to show Mum. "If Gracie had hand-delivered it, she would've hand-*written* it. But this has been printed, which means—"

"—she must have had someone drop it off. A delivery company or something," Iris finished off.

Neither of us said "spook!" – it wasn't the moment for that.

"The girls are right, Suze," said Dad, coming up to Mum and putting an arm around her shoulders as she ran her fingers across the black font of the wording, slightly smudging the ink. "Maybe she ordered it over the phone, or online."

From a really useless company, by the looks of it. The chocolates were the sort you could pick up easily beside the till in Tesco, on special offer. They hadn't even bothered to wrap the box. If I knew where Gracie was or how to get in touch with her, I'd tell her never to order anything from them again. . .

"She *hasn't* been here?" Mum murmured to Dad, her shoulders sinking with the weight of her disappointment.

Iris glanced at me, her eyes wide with worry.

"No, Suze, I don't think so. But then it's great, isn't it?" Dad said gently. "She's thinking about you. About us. She's . . . she's sort of reaching out at last. It's pretty amazing, after, well. . ."

Dad's words tapered off.

After all this time, *after all this silence*, I finished in my head, gazing down again at the tag.

Scanning the letters, I felt a shiver, as if a tiny jolt of electricity had shot through my body. Had anyone else felt that?!

I checked out Mum and Dad, and saw their eyes were locked together, light-bulb bright and sparkling with possibilities.

Iris was biting the nails of one hand at hyperspeed, like a film spooling forward too fast.

Dolly, oblivious to what was going on, was

panting furiously, padding up and down on the spot on her stiff, arthritic paws, infected by the unseen ripple of excitement in the air. Till – oops – she leant sideways against a bush without giving it due consideration and fell right through it.

Six little words, I thought to myself, as I rushed to rescue our dumb old dog.

Six little words (if you didn't count the kisses).

Who knew something so small could jolt us all like an invisible earthquake?

Chapter 7

A head full of yeahs and buts

Iris struck a rock god pose.

The orange glow of the late afternoon sunshine silhouetted her perfectly at the entrance to the café.

"Oh, yes! *Now* you're talking!" she called out, pointing at the dainty speaker in the corner nearest her, where some theme tune to a Disney film was gently tinkling out.

Tossing her hair wildly and thrashing at her air guitar, Iris could have been in serious danger of frightening customers away. Luckily, since it was about five minutes to closing time, the café was mostly empty. Only a dad, finishing his crossword, and his small son, busily pulling the head off his toy robot, were left.

"Good timing, Iris!" Mum called out from behind the counter, where she was tidying up with her new flowery rubber gloves on. "It would be a shame to let the last slice of carrot cake go to waste!"

"Thanks, Suzanne!" said Iris, instantly switching from rock god to hungry teenager. (Yummy Fun was never going to win a prize for being the most cool place that me and Iris could hang out, but it had the advantage of being a) in our local park, and b) where we could always scrounge free food and drinks.)

Iris came weaving between the tables, gratefully grabbed the cake-laden plate Mum held out to her, and crashed down on to the chair next to mine, sending the pages of my homework book fluttering on to my own plate of nearly finished cake.

"Your knee's all better then?" I noted, since there hadn't been a limp in sight during that small blast of posing and weaving.

"What?" Iris blinked blankly at me.

She was always like this. One day she'd be certain that she had swine flu/gastroenteritis/the plague, and the next she'd have forgotten it or moved on to a completely different illness.

"It was squeaking yesterday, remember?" I said, squidging the last few cake crumbs on to my finger and licking them off.

"Oh, *that*!" Iris exclaimed. "No, it's fine. . . Anyway, your mum looks well happy!"

I glanced up and saw Mum wiping down the glass counter, while beaming over at the boy who was now roaring "Off! Off! Off!" as he clattered his toy's head against the edge of the table.

But that's my mum for you – she always has a smile for everyone; for the mums complaining about the lack of froth on their cappuccino, for the toddlers tearing open the sachets of sugar and pouring them over each other.

Of course, her smile today was for a very *particular* reason.

"She's really pleased about that present, isn't she?" said Iris, with a full mouth.

"Yeah . . . but. . ." I answered warily.

Ever since this morning, I'd had a chest full of anxiety and a head full of "yeah . . . *but*. . ."s. Eventually, Mum had had to go and open up at the café, Dad got his stilts out to go off and do his entertaining gig, and Iris headed out to visit her nan. Once I was by myself, I'd tried to play guitar, attempted to do my homework and taken Dolly for a wobble around the block. But then I'd put down the guitar, given up on the homework, laid down the lead and stared instead at the box of chocolates on the kitchen table and thought, "Yeah . . . *but*. . ."

"But what?" Iris frowned at me.

OK, I guessed it was time to focus my "yeah . . . but. . ."s into rational thoughts.

So here was the first one. . .

"Was that present *really* from Gracie?" I muttered quietly.

Iris gave a cough, choking on her cake. "What d'you mean?"

"Well, it was the message, wasn't it?" I replied, passing Iris my glass of water. "I mean, '*With loveness*'? Gracie would *never* write something like that!"

That line was *way* too cutesy for my sister. Gracie was many things: serious, earnest, grouchy and spiky. Gracie did not do cutesy.

"Yes she would!" Iris blurted out a bit too loud for my liking. I mimed at her to turn the volume down, and she continued, in a lower voice. "What about that old Mother's Day card in the living room? The one made of dried macaroni? It's right beside the Fimo frog you made when you were six. It says '*With loveness, Gracie xxx*' inside *that*!"

"Does it?" I said, straining my brain to picture the card amongst the clutter of childhood knick-knacks.

But then I remembered it and my stomach flipped. Iris was right – some younger version of Gracie had made that card for Mum a zillion years ago. How embarrassing that Iris remembered more detail about Gracie than *I* did.

Still there was *another* rational thought that had been bugging me all day. . .

"OK, so maybe she *did* write that once," I said with a shrug, watching as Mum wandered through the large glass doors and began wiping down the tables on the terrace alongside one of her waitresses. "But I'm just really scared."

"About what?" asked Iris, raising her voice, not just cause Mum was safely outside now, but because the little boy was now roaring "Die! Die! Die!" while his dad took not the slightest bit of notice.

"Well, Mum and Dad seem to think the present is a sign that Gracie's coming back."

"They actually *said* that?!" gulped Iris.

"No – actually they said the *opposite* to me," I told her, remembering the chat we'd had at the kitchen table. "Mum and Dad were checking that I wasn't freaked out by the card and stuff. They told me *not* to get my hopes up, but it's not *my* hopes I'm worried about. Knowing them, I *bet* they're expecting her to turn up on the doorstep any second, same as the chocolates. And if she doesn't . . . they're going to be absolutely, totally *gutted*!"

Iris held a forkful of food in mid-air as what I'd said registered.

"I hadn't thought of that!" she murmured, looking shell-shocked. Like Mum and Dad, she'd been swept up by the general wow of the gift.

I wished I could've felt more of the wow and less of the yeah . . . *but*. . . , but I guess that's just the way I am.

Mum and Dad: apart from the blip (the enormous blip) of Gracie going, they're both natural optimists, who always like to say a big "Yes!" to everything, whether it's entertaining at a party for forty squealing kids or leaving Christmas decorations up year-round and using them to raise money for charity.

Gracie is (was?) a natural pessimist, who always liked to say a big fat "No!" to everything, whether it was greenhouse gases or airport extensions or world poverty or whatever other causes her new friends were into, or just a general "No!" whenever I was annoyingly in her orbit.

Me? I'm naturally somewhere in the middle. My Wikipedia entry would start: *Jemima Wisniewski is best known for her quote "Yeah . . . but. . ."*

"Right – are you two done?" Mum's bright voice cut in. "Cause you can help me by stacking the chairs on to the tables so I can mop the floor."

"Of course!" I said brightly back, hoping she hadn't spotted me frowning just now.

Not that she could hear me. The robot-torturing kid had now begun howling as loudly as a fire engine siren, all because his dad was trying to wrestle him into his hoodie so they could leave. I was sure I'd seen or heard that particular siren wail before – but it was probably right here, on some other Sunday while I was trying to do my homework or help Mum tidy up at the end of a shift.

"Thanks, girls!" Mum practically trilled, as she wandered off for the mop, humming happily along to the Disney dirge that was playing.

I had just noisily stacked the first chair when Iris urgently whispered my name.

"Jem!"

She didn't need to say any more; I knew it was best friend code for "Be subtle, but check THIS out!"

And I saw straightaway what she wanted me to check out: a random cute someone in our midst. Only he wasn't that random to *me*.

"Spook!" I squeaked automatically, as I recognized the teenage boy who'd just walked into the café.

He was dressed differently from when I'd seen him last (well, he didn't have that football kit on when I was under the table with him yesterday).

"Hey, Dad!" he called out to the bloke trying to wrangle the roaring kid into the hoodie.

The kid who was now trying to bite his dad; he was the birthday boy from the party. *That's* where I recognized him from!

I could feel a force field of curiosity emanating from Iris, but she knew me too well to ask what I was spooking about yet. Or maybe it was because she'd just noticed me tilting the chair I was holding so that the seat totally obscured my face.

"OK, I've got him; let's just get going," I heard the dad say, above the sound of petulant roaring.

My heart was thundering from embarrassment, or maybe the shock of the coincidence (or more probably both).

Still, with shaking hands, and a shaking chair to

match, I grabbed the opportunity to peek – and saw the boy from under the table heading out of the café door, followed by his flailing little brother, tucked under the restraining arm of his dad.

I was just about to explain who he was, when I saw the boy from under the table stop right by my mum.

He was smiling at her . . . saying something . . . *handing* her something!

And then he turned and walked away, and I was safe to talk – and *breathe*.

"What's that?" I asked Mum, as she walked back into the café.

"Just a flyer – that boy there asked if I'd mind displaying it somewhere. Could you Blu-tack it up beside the poster for the Rock the Park concert?" Mum said the last part of that sentence to Iris, since *her* hands were free and mine were full of chair. "Not that I think he'll get much interest here, I'm afraid! Not many wannabe band members among my mothers and toddlers!"

As Mum laughed and carried on with her tidying, I leant over quickly to read the piece of paper that Iris was holding. And clunked her on the head with the leg of my upside-down chair.

Luckily, she seemed too intrigued by the flyer

to bother with whingeing, or announcing she had concussion.

"Listen to this, Jem!" Iris said excitedly, only giving the side of her head the briefest of rubs. "'Drummer (13) looking to form A BAND. If you are interested, call Max on. . .'"

She fizzled out when she got to the part about the phone number, and just looked up and stared at me.

"Spook!" we both muttered.

Maybe Arnold biting the boy from under the table was all part of one big, mad coincidence that would help us do what we'd always wanted to do – play in something that wasn't just the school orchestra, twanging corny show tunes at the endless end-of-term shows.

"Hey, what are you doing?" I asked, as Iris quickly folded up the flyer and stuck it in her back pocket. Mum had asked her to put it up beside the poster with the rainbow on it, hadn't she?

"No one else needs to see this," said Iris, with shining eyes. "*We're* who that Max is looking for!"

Yeah, I thought, nibbling at my lip. *But only if that rabbit bite doesn't turn septic and Max has to give up playing drums for ever. . .*

Chapter 8

How to spook myself

Hubbub.

It's a funny word, isn't it?

Just the *sound* of it is dumb.

Of course *dictionary*-wise, it means the general chat and murmurings of a crowd.

You know, like in a TV programme or in a film, where there's a random bunch of extras in the background of a scene, all pretending to chat, though you totally sense that they're kicking themselves for not having any *proper* lines to say, like the real actors.

Me and Iris always crack up whenever we spot that. We'll be sitting on the old sofa at my place, or on the slidey leather one at hers, or at the cinema in the back row, and we'll both launch into "blah, blah, blah!" as soon as we spot hubbubing extras. (Yeah, I know it's not so funny for anyone sitting *around* two "blah, blah, blah"ing girls, sniggering so much they're spilling their popcorn.)

There was a hubbub happening now, in the living room.

Only this hubbub wasn't funny.

In fact, it was giving me a knot in my stomach.

My parents; they obviously hadn't heard me come down to the kitchen for a drink, and they didn't know I'd stopped at the bottom of the stairs, catching the murmurings of their voices.

I stood back from the crack of the slightly open door, catching a vertical peek at the cosy scene inside – myriad fairy lights, Mum resting her head contentedly against Dad's shoulder, both of them gazing aimlessly at the fireplace.

And here were snatches of hubbub I could make out.

". . .can't believe she might just. . ."

". . .well, who knows? This *must* mean something. . ."

". . .will she look different, do you. . ."

". . .might seem a lot older to *her*, don't forget. . ."

". . .hey, do you remember that time when she was little and she. . ."

". . .or the time she said to you 'Daddy, do you

know how much'. . ."

I didn't find this particular hubbub much fun, because it meant my parents were doing exactly what I was worried they'd do: getting their hopes up that Gracie was about to follow up her gift drop-off with a personal appearance any second.

OK, OK, if I'm honest it wasn't *just* that. My heart had clunked floorwards cause I'd spotted that they weren't gazing aimlessly at the fireplace; they were staring wistfully at the box of chocolates sitting in pride of place in the middle of the mantelpiece.

What a big kid I am! I thought angrily to myself, hurrying silently up the stairs.

I'd caught myself being jealous that Gracie's present was more important than mine. When I was in the loo a few minutes ago, I saw the diamanté hair combs; they were lying on the bathroom shelf, by the squeezed toothpaste tube, deposited there before Mum took a shower (how very *un*-pride of place).

Yep, I was jealous and sulky; sulky at being sidelined. Me, the reliable one, who smiled, who did well at school, who helped out at the café, who did emergency clown cover. Somehow that meant nothing much compared to the wondrousness of Gracie, even though she'd chosen to go and leave us just because—

Stop! I warned myself.

After walking into my room, I grabbed my guitar from its stand and broke into some nameless loud riff, in an effort to forget about the box in my head; to give the lid a chance to ease its way shut again.

But a few hard-hitting chords in, and a string went *ping*.

I broke off with a sigh, wondering where I'd mislaid my new pack of strings in the general muddle of my room.

And that's when I heard it.

The faint, slightly out-of-tune tinkle of a fairground ride. . .

I padded softly to the window and strained my ears, in case it was the jingle-jangle of a faraway ice-cream van, or some burble of a funfair in a distant park.

Nope. The sounds from outside were of kids thudding a football; a pair of lovey-dovey pigeons cooing on the guttering next door; the reams of Christmas lights gently thwacking together in the evening breeze.

That faint tinkling was coming from somewhere else.

I turned and padded over to my bedroom door, holding my breath to hear better – which made me hear *worse*, since the blood began to pound louder in my ears.

Tinkle-linkle-link!

I yanked the door open.

The hall was quiet and empty.

There were no sounds now – at all. The tinkling had stopped as quickly as it had started.

I let myself breathe again, and ended up panting as hard as Dolly after a brisk walk. Well, after a slow waddle, then.

I don't know what made me think of it, I really don't, but now that I was standing stock-still outside her door, I suddenly had an urge to peek into the forbidden land of Gracie's room again.

And so I turned the handle and pushed.

It didn't budge.

I tried again, uncertain if I'd turned it enough in the first place.

Nothing.

This time, I put my shoulder against the door and

shoved . . . and felt the tiniest bit of give, as if there was a massive weight behind it.

What was *that* about?

With a confused "huh?" ringing in my head, I shoved again – *just* as the immovable object moved, and I went tumbling sideways into the room.

"Hurrumph?" wumphed Dolly, looking as surprised to see me in Gracie's room as I was to see *her* here.

"How did *you* get in?" I asked, as soon as I'd caught my balance.

Stupid question. These days, Dolly could barely understand "walkies", never mind magically develop the power of speech.

But it was bizarre – the door to Gracie's room was always kept shut, except on those days Mum swept in and out for the bedding. And as much as Mum had wanted to go to work and have this be a no-fuss day, there was no way even *she* would do laundry on her birthday.

So how exactly *had* Dolly ended up on this side of the door? Hey, maybe she was the only member of the family who'd inherited Dad's talent for tricks. . .

Whatever, Dolly wasn't about to spill her secrets;

instead she was about to lean happily against my leg.

I let her lean, and gave her a comforting pat. Which gave me a chance to glance around the room again. It looked somehow less strange than it had last night, but I guess the low summer evening light spilling in the window was the reason.

It still looked stark, though, compared to *my* room. Mine was packed with clothes (on the rail, and, er, on the floor), bowls filled with tangled jewellery and mostly used make-up dotted about, books from school and the library and my childhood, plus mounds of mags I should have chucked out but had never got round to.

There was nothing like that here. Apart from the few strands of beads and clump of nail varnishes by the jewellery box, it seemed practically as neat as a B&B bedroom awaiting its next guest. Even the pale mauve walls were neat. Even though I vaguely remembered there once being a corkboard covered in pinned pamphlets and photos and stuff, the only artwork on them now was one big Andy Warhol image of Marilyn Monroe. Gracie had asked for that for her eighteenth birthday. Who knew at the time that she'd only have a few weeks of looking at it before . . . well, let's just stop at before.

"*. . .And it was so sweet that time she. . .*"

A particular chunk of Mum and Dad's hubbub popped into my mind as I stood there, with Dolly gently snoring by my knee.

That had been weird to hear. I mean, this nicer, squishier version of Gracie that my parents reminisced about sometimes . . . was my sister ever really like that? Or was it just Mum and Dad sticking on their rose-tinted glasses *big* time in Miss Grouch's absence? I mean—

Thunk! Thunk, thunk!

"Whumph?!"

Dolly jerked awake, either to the same soft but certain thudding I was hearing, or maybe cause I'd jerked myself round, heart all aflutter, to see where it was coming from.

Thunk! Thunk, thunk!

The window – that's where it was.

On the other side of the glass, a beautiful pale blue butterfly was hurtling itself against the glass, as though the only place it wanted to be was in this room.

"Shoo!" I yelled, worried that it would thunk

itself dead. "SHOO!!"

In the muddle of the moment, it vaguely reminded me of the corny butterflies painted on Gracie's musical jewellery box.

"WHUFF!" Dolly joined in enthusiastically. "WHUFF, WHUFF!!"

"Everything all right up there?" I heard Dad's voice call up from the bottom of the stairs.

"Yep! Fine!! Just Dolly being dopey!!" I yelled back, hastily nudging Dolly out of Gracie's room with my knee.

I pulled the door quickly closed behind me, noticing just before it shut that the butterfly seemed to have realized what windowpanes *were* at last and flown off somewhere less painful.

OK, I told myself firmly. *Stop thinking about Gracie, and STOP spooking yourself!*

I needed to get busy with something else, like finding that packet of guitar strings.

Cause I'd have to practise, and practise *hard*, if I was going to be auditioning for a band soon.

Now *there* was something to make me thrilled and petrified at the same time. . .

Two weeks before the wish

Dolly is sitting directly in front of the TV, her head jerking from side to side, as the camera switches to new angles, and new characters.

With her piggy little eyes, all she can make out – I'm pretty sure – are reasonably interesting blurs.

But me, Iris, Mum and Dad have a perfect view (if you don't count a pair of twitching doggy ears) of Doctor Who, who is about to confront the Alien Ant Queen, or whatever she's supposed to be.

At this point the TV programme makers would probably expect the likes of me and Iris to be hiding behind cushions, holding our breath and hoping the Alien Ant Queen is not about to bite Doctor Who in half and suck out his insides, like she's done to about half the cast in this week's episode already.

Instead, we're fixated on the crowd of terrified citizens hubbubing away in a huddle in the background of the scene.

"Blah! Blah, blah, *blah*!!!" me and Iris are taking turns to say to each other with mock scared expressions on our faces. When we're not sniggering, that is.

"Mum!" says Gracie, suddenly appearing in the living room doorway.

I didn't hear her come in – she's been with her hippy-dippy new mates from The Den again, so you never know what time she's going to get back from *there*. Though how she can want to hang out at a *squat* I don't know. Even if the people living there have hung some curtains up and painted murals round the place, it's still just a semi-derelict building, isn't it? That's what Viv says, anyway. *And* she says she can't understand why Mum and Dad let Gracie go. But try saying no to Gracie about *anything* these days and you get roared at. You practically expect *fire* to come out of her mouth.

At least Dragon Girl's not madly late this time. She came home at nearly one *last* night. I know cause I heard her trying to sneak in (didn't work – not when Dolly started barking, all chuffed to see her), and I heard the row about it with Mum and Dad this morning. ("But darling. . .!" "But I'm nearly *eighteen*!!!")

"Yes, honey?" says Mum now, looking up from the Winnie-the-Pooh characters that she's hand-stitching on to her waitresses' aprons.

"Have you seen yesterday's newspaper?"

"Blah! Blah-blah, blah, blah-blah, blah!" Iris and I carry on with our conversation, in tandem with the hubbubing extras on screen.

"Um . . . I don't know, Gracie," Mum answers, gazing around. "Have you seen it, Owen?"

Dad – in his Normal Person disguise – looks up from the TV. "Nope. What do you need it for, Gracie?"

"Blah, blah, blah?" Iris seems to be asking me, her eyes all cartoon wide.

"Blah, *blah*!!" I reply, to whatever her question was.

"I NEED it," says Gracie, sounding louder than she needs to be, "because— Look! Would you two *SHUT UP* with that blah-blah stuff!!"

Iris and I stop for a second out of sheer surprise – then burst into giggles the second we look at each other.

"Aw, leave Jem and Iris alone," Dad says, smiling indulgently at us. "They're only having a laugh!"

"Yeah?" snaps Gracie, her voice all breakably icy. "Well, not *everyone* in the world has the luxury of having a laugh! Like the Delta tribe that were in yesterday's paper. They're not exactly *laughing*, knowing that multinational oil companies want to—"

"Have you checked the recycling box, honey?" Mum interrupts in her sunniest voice.

Mum's super-sweet and patient, but even *she* can't bear another lecture about environmental issues; not on a Saturday evening after a busy day in the café, when all she wants to do is sit in front of the TV and relax by watching alien ant queens sucking people's insides out while sewing Pooh bears on aprons.

But that's *all* Gracie ever wants to do. I can't even eat my favourite cereal in the morning without her going on about global over-farming of crops. Dad endlessly gets it in the ear about using squirty cream (aerosol: *bad*) for his pie-in-the-face gags. She'd rather read Mum reports on food wastage when she goes to the café than help her clean any up.

Course, Gracie's been into stuff like that *for ever*, but she's got a million times worse since she started going to all those talks and workshops they've started running at The Den. . .

"I've looked already – it's not there," she answers crossly, "and I really want to show this article to Nicko and everyone later, cause they'll be really interested in the campaign for—"

"Blah, blah, blah!" I blurt out.

Oops – didn't mean to say that out loud.

Oops again – it's made *everyone* in the room burst out laughing, *even* though Mum's quickly slapped a guilty hand over her mouth.

"God, sometimes I *hate* this family!!" Gracie growls, leaving the living room with a slam of the door.

"Blah blah-blah blah *blah* blah blah. . ." I mutter under my breath this time, which translates as "And sometimes I *hate* you too. . ."

Chapter 9

The wrong boy (oh boy)

We had a collection of seven flyers in total.

Iris was fanning herself with them, muttering something about how she felt hot and must be coming down with flu.

I knew that what she was *actually* coming down with was an acute attack of nerves. She just didn't have the bottle to make the phone call. But then again, neither did I. . .

"*I* know – toss you for it!" I exclaimed, rummaging in my blazer pocket for a coin.

"No! Er . . . OK. Maybe," Iris waffled.

There was no doubt about it – we were lame, *so* lame.

All we wanted to do was be in a band. Even just have the chance to *audition* to be in a band. We wanted it so badly that we'd talked about nothing else all day at school.

Here's how badly we wanted it: we'd gone on a flyer hunt on our way home in the afternoon, stumbling on one by accident in the newsagent first, and then sussing out that there were probably *more* posted around locally. Displaying amazing powers of cunning and speed, Iris had pulled down flyers that Max had Blu-tacked to windows or walls in the music shop, the post office, the butcher's (!), the florist, Tesco Metro, and the kebab place by the crossing. All while I hovered uselessly, ready to run when she was done.

Which, along with the crumpled one from Mum's café, meant we had *eight* versions of the same phone number that we were too chicken to call.

Whatever, "gathering" up the flyers had used up all Iris's reserve of nerves, and now she was leaning feebly on the railing by the traffic lights, an overheating gibbering wreck. Two old ladies who were standing patiently waiting for the green man gave her a wary glance, probably wondering if she was a thirteen-year-old delinquent about to *mug* them or something.

"Can't *you* just do it, Jem?" Iris suddenly said,

wincing at the sight of the about-to-be-tossed coin in my hand. "I mean, I got all *these*—"

She held up her fan of paper as evidence.

"—and you do sort of *know* Max already. . ."

"My rabbit bit him – it doesn't make us best buddies!" I answered uselessly.

For once I wished I was more like Gracie. Gracie would *never* dither and swither and sweat over anything. Once she'd made up her mind to do something, she just went straight ahead and did it, whether it was decluttering her room, or letting me know exactly how annoying I was, or packing up and—

Don't! I warned myself, and quickly did something to take my mind off the box in my head.

Something a bit scary.

Brrr-brrr. Brrr-brrr. Brr—

"Is it ringing?" Iris asked, her eyes wider than a kid's at a Häagen-Dazs ice-cream counter.

I slapped a hand over the ear that didn't have my mobile pressed to it, half to block out Iris's excited gibbering and half to block out the traffic thundering by.

"*Hello?*" I could just make out the boy's voice say above the background noise.

"Is that Max?!" I asked.

"*Uh-huh*," came a muffled reply.

"Um, this is Jem."

So far, so good. My heart was still thudding around my chest like a big bass drum, but at least I was doing it. Talking to Max, I mean. Without tripping over my words.

"*Who?*"

Aargh! Of course he didn't know my first name! I hadn't told him *that*!

"Wisniewski!" I tried to clarify. And failed.

"What?"

OK, so he'd heard my uncommon surname just once, while under a table (twice, if you count the time our family was in the local newspaper). No wonder he couldn't make it out, with the rumble of buses and cars obscuring it.

"I'm MISS WIGGLE!" I yelled out.

And nearly gave the two shocked old ladies at the lights a heart attack each. . .

"Sounds like a Common Blue," said Iris knowledgeably. "I'll check in a minute. . ."

She was studying the map in the screen of her new phone. After we'd been home to get changed and pick up our guitars, we'd had a bit of a battle about the quickest way to get across town to Max's house, with me wanting to follow the route I vaguely remembered Dad driving on Saturday (though I guess for most of *that* journey I was huddled down in the seat of the van, trying not to make eye contact with the outside world), while Iris wanted to use the map function in her mobile to take a short cut through the housing estate and past the superstore.

The trouble was, I worried that she didn't know how to use her phone properly yet, same as her dad Ray hadn't managed to figure out how to fix the mechanism in the door of their loo. I wasn't even a hundred per cent sure Iris was looking at a map for our *town*.

"So how come you suddenly know about butterflies?" I asked her as we padded on.

I'd been talking to Iris about the pale blue butterfly that had thudded up against Gracie's bedroom window last night. She'd got all excited, wondering aloud if it was some kind of *sign*, rather than just a very stupid insect doing a dumb thing. She couldn't think what sort of sign it was exactly, but I was happy to let her prattle on. I just didn't want to leave any gaps in the conversation so that

I'd have to remember the awfulness of shouting "MISS WIGGLE!" down the phone at a very confused boy. Anyway, because I'd gone purple with embarrassment and lost the power of speech, Iris had done what a best friend should do and saved me, by grabbing the phone and quickly explaining to Max that we'd seen his ad, and we played guitar, and could we audition please, and yes, we'd be at his for 5.30 p.m.

"I did a project on butterflies at my old school, before we moved to Priory Avenue," Iris mumbled in reply to my question, while still staring at her screen. "Anyway, check it out; this alleyway we're on should take us on to his road, right about . . . *now*!"

Yep, we were on a road. With houses. Where Max lived, according to the details he'd given Iris.

Only this *wasn't* the road Dad had parked in on Saturday. And this collection of new houses wasn't *remotely* like the Edwardian terraced house where I'd met Max under the table.

"Are you sure you've got this right?" I mumbled. "Cause this is . . . *wrong*. I haven't been *here* before!"

"No. 12 – it's there, blue door, red car in the drive.

Just like he said!" Iris answered me, sounding wary.

We glanced at each other.

"This is *weird*," I said. "Could be a hoax . . . some lads out to fool people?"

"Or an *older* guy, pretending to be a teenage boy?!" Iris suggested, doing a good job of alarming herself and me.

"Yeah, but it can't be!" I frowned, trying to quash the rising panic and get sensible. "We *saw* Max hand Mum the flyer!"

"So what do we do?" said Iris, with flushed pink cheeks.

I thought for a second, and then came up with a plan.

The plan was hardly ingenious.

All it involved was a) ringing the doorbell, b) running to stand halfway down the path, i.e., well out of harm's way, and c) holding our guitars by the neck, ready to club anyone dodgy.

Luckily, the girl who answered the door looked bored, rather than dodgy.

"Yep?" she yawned, lazily twirling a memory stick that was dangling round her neck. She must have been about nineteen or twenty, and looked effortlessly cool, in denim cut-offs and some old, faded logo T-shirt.

"Is Max in?" me and Iris asked in unison, like schoolgirl Tweedledees and Tweedledums. Neither of us said "spook!" – the older girl was already eyeing us up dubiously as it was.

"Yep," she answered in that same faintly bored tone. "Come in. . ."

We came, gazing around a reassuringly normal hall, with a reassuringly ordinary kitchen up ahead, with a laptop and textbooks piled on it.

"He's in his room – as usual," said the girl.

She tilted her head towards the stairs and rolled her eyes. The gesture seemed faintly familiar for a second. Not that I had any time to think about why that might be.

"Maxie!! Oi – MAXIE!!" the girl yelled, walking backwards towards the kitchen. "Oh, just go up – he's got his headphones on, probably. His is the door at the top of the stairs. . ."

As the older girl padded off back to her work, there didn't seem anything to do except do as she said.

And so a whole three seconds later, we found ourselves standing outside an open bedroom door, staring – oh boy – at a *complete* stranger.

A completely strange, slightly chunky, messy-haired boy who was lolling on a battered sofa, pulling faces as he played *Guitar Hero* on his Wii.

The boy-who-wasn't-Max must have sensed us standing there – he whipped round and yanked his headphones off, letting the faint hiss of some heavy metal track buzz in the background.

"Yeah?" he said defensively, getting to his feet. With his startled eyes, he reminded me a bit of a hamster I used to have. It had a spiky, goldie tuft of fur on the top of its head too.

Me and Iris; neither of us spoke, waiting for the other, so we didn't repeat the Tweedledee and Tweedledum thing again. Which of course resulted in an awkward dollop of silence.

"We're—" we both gave in and said together, then stopped.

"Looking for Max," I finished off alone, staring at the wrong Max, as Iris pulled out a fistful of flyers to illustrate the point.

"He put these up."

"*I'm* Max," said the flustered boy. "My friend Ben went round with those for me."

Clunk.

Things fell into place straightaway – it made

sense of the wrong road, the wrong house, the wrong Max.

And why the boy didn't understand a word of my waffle about Wisniewski and Wiggle earlier on.

"Is Ben in the band too?" I asked tentatively, hopefully.

"Nah," the wrong Max answered, now trying to sound as flat and bored as his sister in an attempt to regain his cool. "He's not into music. Not playing, anyway."

Neither are you, I thought to myself.

Me and Iris had a thing about *Guitar Hero*; a snobby thing. We just didn't get why anyone would want to faff around doing a fancy version of air guitar when you could play a real one for, er, real.

More importantly, the flyer had said *Drummer (13) looking for band.* So where was the drum kit? I couldn't see one anywhere in this untidy room. And when you think about it, they're pretty hard-to-hide bits of musical equipment.

"So, should we . . . um . . . play you something?" I heard Iris suggest to Max, and saw her fidget with the zip of her guitar case.

"Yeah, whatever," the tufty-haired boy said in a

couldn't-care-less sort of voice.

He took one hand out of his skater shorts pocket and waved vaguely at a messy old sofa in the corner of his room, like he was unenthusiastically inviting us to sit there.

But before me and Iris had a chance to shuffle over, the wrong Max did something *very* bizarre.

"*Unnngh!!*" he suddenly bellowed, then made a *lunge* at the sofa.

Confused by the caveman roar, it took a second for me to notice what he grabbed from there.

And then, *yuck* . . . I spied a pair of *boxers* clutched in his hand!

I was too stunned to say a thing. Same went for Iris. In fact, the silence was deafening.

I mean, what do you say in an unexpected pants moment?

The wrong Max certainly didn't speak a word – just opened a drawer and stuffed his crumpled underwear in there.

The next sound I heard was Iris carrying on unzipping her guitar case. I guess she thought that music might cover up the looming awkwardness. And so I copied her, and in a few short seconds later we were strumming in tandem, not daring to look at each other, *or* the wrong Max.

Our piece ended.

More silence.

The wrong Max didn't utter a single mutter.

Maybe it was because we'd only done one verse and a chorus of The Beatles' "Here Comes The Sun". Maybe the wrong Max expected us to play the whole thing. Or sing, maybe. But neither me nor Iris had thought to do that. Or maybe he hated The Beatles, like Gracie.

"Um . . . that's it," I said, as I began shoving my guitar back in its case, trying not to scoop up a stray sock along with the strap. (*Ewww. . .*)

"Mmm . . . yeah, thanks," the wrong Max finally muttered, ruffling up his tousled hair and addressing his words to the view out of his window. "Got your, uh, number."

Quickly, and very willingly, Iris and I trundled back down the stairs we'd come up all of four minutes before.

Blam!

And so ended our first ever tryout for a band – with a bang of the front door behind our backs.

"Well, *that* was lousy!" I exclaimed, relieved to be in the fresh air. "He was so *rude*!"

"Look on the bright side," Iris grinned at me.

"Which is?" I said, hiking my guitar case up on to my back.

"We could get in the record books for the shortest *ever* audition!"

Giggling, we set off down the path – till I stopped dead.

"Anna Willis!" I suddenly blurted out.

"Huh? Who's Anna Willis? That girl, you mean? Max's sister?"

I turned and stared back at the house, as if I had X-ray vision and could see the girl in the cut-offs, sitting scowling over her coursework while miserable Max went back to twiddling with his pretend guitars.

"She was at sixth form with Gracie for a while. . ." I said, remembering the face, only with a different hairstyle and more spots disguising it.

"Really?" said Iris. "Spook!"

It was then that I realized quite how many "spook!"s seemed to be going on in my life over the last few days.

What did it mean?

Did it mean anything at all?

Did it mean I was the magnet for some strange,

otherworldly weirdness?

Or that I was going slightly mad around the edges?

Hmm. Maybe I should keep a note of all the spooks that have happened and try to make sense of them that way, I thought to myself.

"Hey, how about we write all these spooks down?" Iris said out loud.

Spook!

Chapter 10

Loud, wet and dangerous

Dolly sat in front of us, loyally barking the baddies away.

All around us was mayhem – like a fearsome battle scene being played out with giggles and water bombs.

But for the moment, the traditional last-day-of-term soak-a-thon in the park involving about half (the idiot half) of our school had missed us.

Me, Iris and Dolly sat on the sanctuary of the Yummy Fun café steps, finishing our free milkshakes (not Dolly – bad for her elderly digestion). Inside the café, the kiddy entertainer Jeff was singing his awful collection of nursery rhymes to the squealing toddlers and their doting mothers.

Also inside – tucked safely away from water bombs and sticky kiddie fingers in the back office – were our guitars. We'd done our music teacher, Mr Steed, proud (and made ourselves feel faintly ashamed) by cracking through a bunch of creaky old rock tracks in the end-of-term show this afternoon, along with the rest of the long-suffering school orchestra.

And here we were, free for six whole weeks.

Free to avoid helping Dad out at any more parties if I could possibly avoid it, since Spike had definitely handed in his notice and started working at the computer store (boo).

And free to do . . . well, probably nothing much of *anything*, I didn't suppose, now our dreams of being in a cool band were over.

"OK," Iris began, tapping her pencil on the open page in her notepad, "so *excluding* general, run-of-the-mill 'spook!'s like—"

"Saying things together," we both said together.

"It goes like this," Iris continued on her own. "*Number one: Seeing Gracie's reflection in the glass panels by your door on Saturday morning. . .*"

I held my hand out flat and wobbled it, uncertain that this first point counted. (Dolly reached over and sniffed my hand experimentally.) "Not sure about *that*; it was just *me* seeing myself, after all," I said.

"Sorry, but that's a 'spook!' as far as I'm concerned," Iris replied matter-of-factly, "cause there was *more* Gracie-ness later on. Which brings us on to the *next* point . . . see?"

She turned the notepad around towards me, so I could read her neatly set out words. (Dolly sniffed that experimentally too.)

Under a title – *Spooks!!* – and the first entry, the list continued.

2. Same day, *you help your dad out at a party and meet Ben*, *who mentions that he remembers seeing your family talking about Gracie in the newspaper.*

3. You see a place card with her name on.

4. A kid comes up and strokes Arnold – her name is Gracie.

5. You hear weird music, *and go into Gracie's room—*

"Yeah, but I don't know if I *really* heard something or just dreamt it," I protested, pointing to number five.

"*Dolly* seemed desperate to get into her room, remember, so it counts as a 'spook!', absolutely. And check out number seven – you thought you heard something on Sunday night as well!"

I glanced back at her list.

6. The boy you met at the party comes into the café with a flyer for a band.

7. You think you hear the weird music again, and go back into Gracie's room, where Dolly is stuck!

8. A butterfly flies into the window—

"That made me *jump*; it wasn't a proper 'spook!'," I interrupted, tapping on the latest point. Though even as I said it, my mind did a game of match-up, throwing up images of the dusty blue butterfly at the glass and the crudely painted cobalt ones dotted around Gracie's music box. . .

"No – we're definitely keeping that one. Why would a butterfly *do* that, and right at the moment you're in the room?" asked Iris, in a voice that sounded like she was enjoying the drama, and wasn't really expecting an answer. "And finally number nine: we go to the wrong Max's house, which is a *disaster*, BUT you recognize his sister, who's an old friend of Gracie's. Now isn't that THE most amazing pattern of coincidences?!"

"Well, yeah," I admitted. After all, the overload of coincidences was the whole reason I'd sat down with Iris to make a list of all the "spook!"s this week.

But she seemed to have missed out the biggest "spook!" of all.

"What about the present that Gracie left for Mum?!"

Iris shrugged when I spoke, and squirmed a bit. She knew she'd goofed by missing that out, I was sure. But she didn't seem about to admit it.

"That's not a proper 'spook!' though, is it? I mean, it's *special*, but it's not a 'spook!' Your mum getting a present on her birthday . . . that wouldn't be a surprise, *technically*, would it?"

I was incredibly stunned at Iris's train of thought. I mean, how could she not see that it was pretty surprising – *spookily* surprising – for Mum to get a present from Gracie of all people, after two missed Mum birthdays (*and* mine, *and* Dad's), and after 941 days of never getting in touch?

I didn't get the chance to say all that, though, because we suddenly got caught in the very wet crossfire of a bunch of Year Ten boys and girls squirting each other with water bottles filled at the fountain.

"Wuff!" barked an indignant Dolly, as she took an unexpected shower.

"Let's go!" Iris urged, motioning for me to follow her back inside the café.

I nearly went for it, till I squinted through the

plate-glass window and saw that Jeff had got his bubble machine out, which always turned the little kids completely crazy. They were already leaping and clapping and clattering into each other with shrieks of joy and howls of pain.

"Or how about we escape through the bushes," I suggested instead.

Iris nodded, now that she'd spotted how loud, wet and dangerous things had got both inside the Yummy Fun as well as out.

We slunk round the back of the café, dragging Dolly behind us. Bending down, me and Iris squirmed our way through the tangle of rhododendrons (it was a lot easier and took less bending when we were small and seven and first knew each other) till we emerged into the relative tranquillity of the old rose gardens.

"Wuff!" Dolly barked at a nearby bin.

"Shush!" I told her, giving her a comforting, rough rub of the back.

Luckily, most of the end-of-term water fights hadn't made their way round here yet – there was just one group of Year Sevens mucking about over by the lily pond.

Still, if they saw us (alerted by Dolly's barking)

then we *might* become prime targets for plastic cupfuls of green, sludgy, pond-weedy water.

"Where should we—"

Iris's question didn't get answered, because we both suddenly heard something.

A *song* something.

"What *is* that again?" I whispered, as we both concentrated on the sweet, woody-sounding vocals and where they might be coming from. "Wait . . . isn't it—"

"—Kasabian?!" Iris finished for me, holding her breath as much as I was to be sure not to miss a note.

We were thinking the same thing: how strange it was to hear the shouty lads' rock of "Fire" sung like some sweet, melodic ballad. No wonder it had taken us a few seconds to recognize it.

And then I noticed that neither of us was holding on to Dolly's lead. . .

"Uh-oh. Where's Dol—" I began in a flap, till I spotted her short, stubby wagger of a tail disappearing around the side of the nearby park gardeners' shed, which presumably contained lawnmowers, copious amounts of shears, hoses and seeds, and whatever else gardeners might fancy keeping in their sheds.

"Dolly?" I called softly, keeping my voice and myself low, so as not to attract the unwanted attentions of the Year Sevens by the pond.

"Jem!" hissed Iris, coming up hard behind me and grabbing my arm so I couldn't move forward. "Listen!"

I listened.

And the singing became clearer, now that we were closer to the source.

Which is exactly where *Dolly* was, apparently.

Me and Iris took a step forward and peeked around the corner of the building – at the exact moment the singing stopped.

Which is when – spook! – we both saw the wrong Max take his earphones out and stare in confusion as Dolly settled herself for a snoozy lean against his knees.

It had been him *singing?!* I could practically hear Iris thinking to herself, since that was what I was thinking too.

His voice was good – really good!

Of course, at that moment, the wrong Max glanced around for the owner of the strangely leaning dog.

And of course, me and Iris were too spooked by

the sight of him to jump back around the corner quickly enough.

"Oh!" the wrong Max squeaked, jerking in shock as if we'd just slapped him.

And in the bright sunshine on that Friday afternoon (instead of the subterranean gloom of his bedroom on Monday teatime), I instantly realized that we *weren't* in the presence of a big-headed, way-too-cool wrong boy.

From the luminous strawberry flush of his cheeks – his whole head and *neck*, even – I knew this person was just deeply, HUGELY—

"Hey! Did you two take all my ads down?!" he suddenly asked, sounding defensive.

Instantly I backtracked, swallowing the word "shy".

"Uh, yes. . ." muttered Iris. "Sorry. How do you know?"

"My mate Ben just phoned and said all the flyers he'd put in shops had vanished. And his uncle in the butcher's said he saw two girls making off with the one that had been in *his* window."

It was on the tip of my tongue to point out that having an ad for a band in a butcher's was a lousy bit of marketing anyway (same went for a kiddy café and most of the rest of the places Ben had placed Max's band ads).

But instead, I found myself saying, "Are you mad at us?"

"Uh, no, not really," he muttered back. "The thing is, I don't think I could. . ."

The rest of his words were lost in a fuzz of mumbled words.

"What?" I pressed him, edging nearer, so I could grab Dolly's lead if nothing else.

"I said I don't think I could go through that again," the wrong Max muttered a little louder, directing the words at his knees.

"Go through *what* again?" asked Iris, getting brave and flopping herself down beside him on the patchy grass by the shed wall.

"Auditions. They're too . . . *hard*."

Hard? I thought to myself. *For us? Or for him. . .?*

Iris and I glanced at each other. Was the wrong Max saying what we *thought* he was saying? That we *scared* him? *Us*?

Ha!

OK, so I was right. The wrong Max really was genuinely, painfully shy.

"You, er, sing really well," I told him truthfully,

hoping a compliment might make him feel less awkward with us.

It worked, sort of.

"You both, er, play really well," the wrong Max told his knees, rather than us.

Whatever, knees or not, that was *it*.

None of us realized at that second, but a couple of errrr'd compliments had changed everything.

"Wuff!" barked Dolly, waking up instantly from her nano-sleep against the wrong Max's legs.

Wuff indeed.

We were – from that pink-cheeked, mega-cringey moment on – a real, live *band*. . .

Chapter 11

Well, hello (again)

OK, so we were a real live band *sort of*.

There were a few teething problems to sort out. For a start, we had no name, no songs we could agree on, and Iris and I had never heard Max play a single note of any instrument. (Oops.)

On the *plus* side, it was early days; we'd only hooked up in the park with Max yesterday afternoon, and he was coming around to mine at four o'clock today for our first ever band meeting, to play around with possible band names and songs and rehearsal plans. (How funny – when I gave him the address, he asked what colour front door we had, to help him spot the place. Like you'd have any trouble picking it out from all the other houses in the street! But just so he could get the full effect of the surprise, I told him "red", and nothing else. Ha!)

It was only mid-morning now, and after mooching around in my bedroom for an hour or so, me and Iris were padding down the stairs, aiming to go rifle in the fridge for snacks.

"*I* know!" I heard Iris's mum's voice drift from the kitchen. "This band the girls have joined; maybe they could play at the—"

CREAK! went the sound of ten tiny doors opening, and Viv paused, letting ten tiny birds come out and cuckoo the time.

"—street party!" Viv finished off once the kitchen was quiet again.

"*What* street party?" Iris asked, as we wandered into the room.

While I'd been getting changed upstairs, Iris had lain on my bed, scribbling *10. Bump into Max in the park – and he's not a doofus after all!* on to our "spook!" list.)

Mum and Viv seemed to have been busy scribbling things too. On the kitchen table in front of them was an A4 notepad, covered in scrawled red bullet points and wording plus masses of doodles.

"Viv says some of the neighbours have been talking about having a big street party during the holidays, so we're getting a few ideas together!" said Mum, her eyes twinkling.

Like I said, she and Dad are the sort of people hard-wired to say "Yes!" to everything. And now here she was, all fired up with an injection of possible-ness since Gracie's present arrived, and it looked like she was about to throw herself into a brand new project, with gallons of oomph.

"That'd be fun," I nodded, leaning on Mum's shoulders and glancing down at the scribbles and doodles. "But since our band's existed for. . ."

I looked over at Iris, who was better than me at mental arithmetic.

"Eighteen hours," she calculated instantly.

". . .eighteen hours, then I think it's safe to say that we won't be *quite* ready to perform at it!"

"Course you will!" said Viv brightly. "It's not going to be for a few weeks! And we'll get your dad to wander round doing balloon animals for the kids, and your mum will do the catering – it'll be a real family affair!"

"Where *is* Dad?" I asked, thinking I hadn't seen him for a bit.

"Out in the workshop," said Mum, nodding her head in the direction of the giant shed at the bottom of our garden, otherwise known as Mr Wiggle's HQ. "I think he said he had to superglue some plastic spiders to a vest for a new trick he wants to try ou—"

BING BONG!!

"WUFF! WUFF! WUFF!" barked Dolly, going doolally at the sound of the doorbell.

She got up stiffly and directed her barking at the door. Unfortunately it was the back door.

"This way, Dolly!" I told her, nudging her gently around and leading her along the hallway towards the *front* door.

We all missed the smart, bouncy dog we used to have, but the old, crazy one was pretty lovable too. The dementia had started creeping in about a year ago, when Dolly would wake up from a nap, stretch herself, and walk purposefully towards somewhere or other. She'd then stop dead, mid-step, completely forgetting what doggy deeds she'd planned to do. Now, along with the leaning and snoozing, she'd developed some other nuts but intriguing habits, like growling at cushions and licking snails.

And now she was going to do her stranger-at-the-door trick, which consisted of barking fiercely at whoever was on the doorstep, then immediately going and sitting on their shoes the minute the door opened.

"Shush, Dolly!" I urged her uselessly, as I pulled on the latch.

And found myself looking at Max.

Who looked a little bit like he'd just found himself beamed into space. (Our front garden has that effect on people.)

"Max?" I said, since he seemed incapable of speech. "You're a bit early!"

"Jem?" he said, frowning at me.

Wow, the sight of all the Christmas decorations must have *really* fried his brains.

"Like six hours early," I told him, holding out my arm so he could see my watch.

"Huh?" Max mumbled, his face as red as our front door. "Oh! I had the *dentist* at ten, and *you* at four! I got it the wrong way round!"

So Max's brain was in a knot even *before* he saw our Christmas decorations. Still, the way he was staring at me was slightly freaking me out. What was with that?

"Do you want to come in anyway?" I offered. "Iris is here. But it'll have to be quick, cause I'm going out with my dad in a minute. . ."

"Uh, yeah," said Max, trying to take a step inside, which was difficult when you have a stocky dog sitting on your trainers. "Like your new hairstyle!"

Aaarghhh. . .!

Now he'd stopped staring and started joking. And *now* I'd realized I'd answered the door in my apprentice clown costume, complete with purple afro and red nose.

"Thought this might work as our band look," I joked back, glad once again to have thick white make-up covering up my blushes. . .

Max was wearing my nose.

"It suits you!" I called over, as I tried not to wobble Arnold around too much inside her gold box.

I was heading across the bowling green grass, about to put our bunny safely back in the van now that the party had ended.

The only answer Max could manage was a grin – he had more small children hanging off each limb than seemed physically possible.

As for Iris, well, she'd put herself in charge of the bubble machine, and was jumping around with a bunch of kids, catching more bubbles than a supposedly cool teenage girl should do.

When me and Dad had arrived at the old bowling green in the park a couple of hours ago, my heart had soared when I saw how pretty it looked; the parents of the birthday girl had hung flowery bunting and balloons all over the old wooden pavilion, and dragged tables outside that were covered in bright polka-dotted tablecloths and cake stands piled high with pastel cupcakes.

But my gladdened heart took a nosedive when I'd spotted Iris and Max twenty minutes into Dad's act, leaning on the fence that looped around the bowling green, gawping and giggling at the free show.

I'd tried to frown at Iris, to show her I wasn't thrilled that she'd schlepped Max here, but with a red banana smile painted on, it's kind of hard to register grumpiness.

Still, hurray for Dad; he wasn't about to give them a free ride.

"I need a couple of volunteers for my next trick," he'd called out, and a flurry of small hands flew in the air. "Ah, yes – you two by the gate; come on in!"

He ushered Iris and a suddenly mortally shy Max to come forward, and within thirty seconds had a giggling Iris inside the ostrich costume and Max wearing a pink tutu over his skater shorts, in front of a gaggle of hysterical children.

For a second, I'd thought Max was about to burst a blood vessel, his face was so red with shame. My own embarrassment popped like a burst bubble and I felt a sudden, overpowering wave of pity.

"Here," I said, hurrying over to him and taking my red clown nose off. His eyes were full of quiet panic. "Wear this and make 'em laugh!"

"D'you think?" he mumbled, worriedly.

"Absolutely!" I reassured him, honking his nose for luck.

It seemed to work. The second I stepped away, ready to get the props for Dad's next magic trick, I saw Max give a cartoon curtsy, holding the edges of his tutu. The kids erupted – and Max smiled. (Phew.)

He hadn't stopped smiling since, and instead of slinking away at the earliest opportunity, he'd stuck around and laughed along with Iris at the rest of the show, helped load Dad's van, and was amusing the last of the kids waiting to be picked up by turning himself into a human climbing tree.

"Here, Jem – *I'll* take Arnold," said Dad, gently relieving me of the box. "Do you want to chuck your gear in the back of the van and just hang out with your friends?"

The afternoon had been more fun than I thought it would be, but getting out of the afro and the stripy dungarees was pure pleasure.

"Is it all gone now?" I asked Iris five minutes later, as we strolled over towards the play park.

"Just a bit beside your ear. Here, let me," said Iris, taking the wipe from my hand and stopping to clean off the last of my make-up.

Max hovered beside us, but his gaze was on the screen of his mobile rather than on the missed splodges of make-up on my face, or the swings where we were headed.

"My mate Ben's going to meet us here," Max mumbled, reading from a text that had just bleeped through. "He says he's just near the park entrance."

So we were going to be meeting Ben! Under-the-table, flyer-posting, cute-looking, not-Max Ben!!

Iris's eyes met mine, and we gave each other the faintest "oo-er!" smile; a smile so small that anyone else might have described it as a tiny facial twitch.

We were so lost in that secret smile that we didn't notice Max grinding to a halt by a tree and nearly bumbled right into him.

"Look," he said, pointing to a familiar poster with a rainbow on it. "The Rock the Park concert they're holding here . . . *anyone* can enter it. Maybe we could do that *next* year!"

"Why next year? We could do it *this* year!" said Iris brightly.

I knew she still had the "spook!" book in her bag, ready to add more "spook!"s whenever they might happen. I saw her whip it out now, turn to the back, and scribble down the contact number for the concert organizer.

"Nah – it's happening in a couple of weeks' time, and we'll have to rehearse for *months*," muttered Max, his cheeks pinking up at the thought of performing.

OK, so I had to remind myself that Max was too shy even to hand out his own flyers, so it was no surprise that he was silently freaking at the idea of playing in front of real, live people. Me and Iris, on the other hand, were old pros when it came to doing gigs. Even if they *were* just in front of the rest of the school and parents, or the residents of the local retirement home, or other equally non-glamorous audiences.

"We'd be fine! It's the holidays now – we can rehearse every single day, if we want. We're not busy doing anything else!" I pointed out, while secretly praying that Dad didn't get any more big party bookings that he'd need me to assist at.

"Yeah, but—" Max began to protest (sounding suddenly like me).

He didn't get any further than that, thanks to being suddenly bundled to the ground from behind.

"*OOOF!!*"

Why do boys like to do that to their mates? Jump on their backs, I mean? And if they're not saying hello by jumping on their backs, they're punching each other's arms.

"Hey, Ben! *Ouch!*" Max winced happily, as the dark-haired boy helped him back to his feet and then thumped him on the bicep. "This is Jem and Iris – the girls I was telling you about."

"Yeah," Max's friend replied with a knowing grin. "The ones who nicked the flyers I put up!"

Well, hello (again), I thought. He didn't recognize me from his brother's party last week, I was pretty sure.

"Uh, Max," the boy called Ben continued, suddenly switching his attention back to his friend. "Did you know you had some foam and a plastic spider in your hair?"

"Do I. . .?" muttered Max, rubbing the back of his head, where he'd been "pied" earlier. "I crashed a kids' party over by the old bowling green. The children's entertainer—"

"—was my dad," I interrupted, thinking I might as well mention the connection. "I'm Miss Wiggle . . . hope you didn't need a tetanus jab for the bite my rabbit gave you last Saturday!"

That was pretty funny. That covered up my shyness pretty well, I reckoned.

"Ah, OK!" blurted Ben, nodding and smiling broadly. "So *you're* the girl under the table, right?!"

Max looked at us both, confused. "Ah! You're the girl Ben was talking about – from his brother's party?"

Uh-oh. Wish I was wearing my clown make-up – just to hide my mega-blush.

Ben had been talking about me?!?

Don't get excited, I warned myself. *He wasn't necessarily telling Max good stuff. He probably did say I reminded him of a lunatic killer clown from a horror movie.*

He wasn't looking at me like I was a freak right now, though. He was looking at me in a way a boy hadn't ever before. In a way that made my tummy lurch and my heart speed up alarmingly.

"Uh, yep," I muttered, sounding less funny and confident now.

"D'oh!" Max exclaimed, hitting himself on the forehead. "Ben was on about a girl clown, and then there you are, working for your dad today. Why didn't I *get* that you were the same person?"

(Whoah, Max's friend was still gawping at me. This was totally weirding me out.)

"It's an easy mistake to make!" Iris chipped in brightly, as she pushed open the gate that led to the swings. "There are *so* many thirteen-year-old girl clowns around, obviously!"

Now *that* was funny. I wished *I'd* come out with that. But the way Ben was staring and smiling at me, I wasn't sure I'd be able to do anything except stammer if I tried to reply.

"So . . . how did your first band meeting go, then?" asked Ben.

He was quite tanned, probably from playing a lot of football, I thought, remembering the kit he was wearing when he walked into Mum's café. Max had more of a bedroom tan; i.e., pasty white, from playing too much *Guitar Hero*.

And while Ben seemed football-fit and lean, Max reminded me again of that old hamster I had, who preferred snoozing in his exercise ball rather than running around in it.

"Well, we're just about to have it, actually," Max told him, as he wandered over and settled himself on a free swing.

"Yeah, but the good news is that we've probably got our first gig!" laughed Iris, plonking herself on the swing to the left of Max and tapping a finger on the notebook.

"No, we're not def—"

"It's the Rock the Park thing. You maybe, um, saw the posters around?" I said to Ben, managing to control my voice, I was pleased to see. "*And* we might do the street party that's happening in our road too."

"The *what*?" Max asked, sounding alarmed.

"Wow! That's so cool!" said Ben, ignoring his friend and keeping his eyes locked on me.

Wow, it is incredibly unnerving to have a cute boy stare at you, specially when it's the first time ever. For something to do, I went over and settled myself on the empty swing to the right of Max.

"Yeah, it'll be fun!" I tried to answer him in a casually confident voice that came out a bit shriller than I'd have liked. I began to swing lazily, to cover up the fact that I felt completely flustered.

"Can't wait to see you guys playing," Ben said, circling around us, scuffing the toe of his trainer on the soft play park surfacing.

"Course we'll have to practise loads," I said, swinging myself a little higher. "Don't want everyone booing us offstage!"

OK, it was much easier to talk normally now that I wasn't directly in Ben's eyeline.

"Well, that's never going to happen, is it?" I heard him say, from somewhere behind me. "Max is a really great singer and drummer. And if you two are as good as he says you are, then I bet all it would take is a few rehearsals to get a couple of songs ready to play!"

Urgh. Was I destined to out-blush Max today? At least *this* time the flushed face was because of a compliment.

I swung higher, looking at the tops of the trees and the clouds, letting the breeze cool my cheeks.

"Fancy a *PUSH*!" I heard Ben call out *just* before I was hurled high enough to make me squeal like a very girly girl.

"EEK!! *Stop!*" I yelled, though I was loving every delicious, unexpected second of being flung into the sky by a very cute boy-from-under-the-table.

In the seconds that I swung back down past her,

I saw Iris giving me that barely visible best friend smile/facial tic, while all I saw of Max was a blur of tufty hair.

And on the way back up was the sun, and the fluffy clouds, and the faraway rooftops beyond the park.

Freeze-frame.

If it was possible to stop that moment dead – the moment I was at the highest arc of the swing – this is what the image would be: a startled girl, suspended in space, her eyes suddenly fixed on the top floor of a dilapidated, semi-derelict red-brick building.

Once upon a time, it had been a school, but more lately, a couple of years ago at least, it had been a squat, with a swirly hand-painted sign at the end of the lane that led to it. The sign – long painted over – had said *All Welcome at The Den*.

And as the girl frozen in time looked over at the crumbling chimney stacks of the building, a dusty blue butterfly fluttered and danced over the uppermost leaves of the sycamores.

Spook! thought the girl, who was me, swinging back down to earth with her heart thumping madly. . .

One month before the wish

"Close your eyes! No peeking!" says Mum.

Her hands are over Gracie's eyes.

Outside, fat clouds seem full of snow; inside, a fire is crackling in an ornate cast iron fireplace.

"Mum, I'm not five!" Gracie laughs, though it's one of her laughs with a sharp, impatient edge to it.

Yeah, yeah, we *know* she's not five any more – for the last year, all we've heard is "Look! I'm *nearly* eighteen!! Leave me alone!" about a million times a week. Now, finally, she's actually *is* eighteen, as of today. Maybe that'll make her happy. Maybe it means she'll give the arguing a rest.

I *wish*. . .

Anyway, Gracie's birthday is why we're all here for a meal in the cosy restaurant at the back of the Rose & Crown pub. Though you get the feeling that Gracie wishes we hadn't bothered. Well, not so much a feeling – it's more the fact that she'd said, "I wish you hadn't bothered" before we left the house. Mum and Dad asked her to invite a couple of her girlfriends along too (I remember *lots* of birthday bowling parties or days out to theme parks where Francine or Becci or both would be glued to Gracie's side) but she said no, she didn't see much of the girls any more. So Mum and Dad asked if she wanted to invite one or two of her *new* friends (our parents are trying, they're *really* trying), but Gracie just rolled her eyes and snorted.

So the celebration "gang" today consists of Gracie, Mum and Dad and me, plus Iris and her parents Viv and Ray, to make up numbers and add a bit of oomph to the happy birthday song, I guess.

Which is about to happen any second. Dad got up from the table and went somewhere about five minutes ago, and Gracie knows as well as everyone else that he's in the pub kitchen, lighting candles on the cake that he or Mum must've stowed there earlier.

"Oh . . . my . . . *gosh*!!" gasps Viv, who has a clearer view of the door to the kitchen than the rest of us.

"What? What!!" Gracie asks, sounding slightly panicked.

Now I can see what's coming too – and so can every other Sunday lunch customer in the restaurant area.

Oohs and aahs and gasps and giggles are rippling from tables all around. People in the main part of the pub are peering through the open double doors too, sensing that something quite special might be happening.

And the special thing is a clown on a unicycle, carrying a bunch of helium balloons and a giant pink cake blazing with candles, accompanied by another, younger, gawky-looking clown holding an accordion.

Keeping his balance by rolling back and forth on the spot, Dad/Mr Wiggle gives Mum the nod, and – amazingly – his red nose starts flashing (must be a new toy he's got). Following the rhythm of the flashing, an awkward-looking Spike begins to creak out the birthday song on the accordion, just as Mum gets ready to whip her hands away from Gracie's eyes.

She's not going to like this, I know it for a fact.

She's not going to like the fuss and the attention.

She's not going to like everyone in the whole place staring and pointing, even if they *have* all joined in singing her "Happy Birthday".

I almost feel sorry for her. I mean, when will Mum and Dad learn that Gracie just *doesn't* like all the cartoon silliness we live with? It's never suited her. It's like forcing a nun to join a street dance troupe and expecting her to join in with all the "Yo!"ing and back flips.

But then I feel sorry for Mum and Dad too. All they've ever wanted is to make things special for both of us. For Dad in particular – who brightens people's days *every* day – it must be hard to accept that Gracie actually prefers to see the world in black and white and shades of grey. . .

Gracie stares, pink-cheeked and smile-free, first at Dad, and then positively *glowers* at poor, shuffling Spike, and back again.

As the last line of the song warbles to a close, I swap glances with Iris. Her mouth is smiling but her eyes are worried. She knows what I'm thinking.

Just be nice, Gracie, for Mum and Dad's sake, I mutter to myself. *This can be your last family birthday if you want it to be . . . you don't have to be around this time next year if that's what you want.*

This time next year, she'll be away at university studying bio-environmental-something-or-other. This time next year, she can celebrate her birthday by hanging out with similarly earnest student mates, or by campaigning against landfill sites or by going on a hunger strike in protest against deforestation in Botswana or whatever else my no-fun-zone sister fancies doing.

But just this once, this one last time, can she fake a smile and say thanks to Mum and Dad? Can she blow out the candles like it's not a chore, and eat the cake without mentioning the evils of processed flour? Can she open her gifts (a Warhol print of Marilyn Monroe; an iPhone; a new bottle of DKNY perfume, since I accidentally tipped her old bottle over when I was trying to stop Dolly flailing around the bathroom when I was giving her a bath) with a bit of enthusiasm?

No.

"Back in a minute," Gracie says, getting up from her chair as the waves of applause ebb away. And with that she's stomped off to the loos without even stopping to make a wish (though I know what her wish would be – she's mumbled it under her breath often enough).

"Well!" roars Ray, good-naturedly. "Think I'll have to borrow that nose of yours, Owen. Should make my next office meeting a *lot* less gloomy!!"

We all smile and laugh a little too loudly, to cover up for the fact that there are now two redundant clowns and an unwanted candle-covered cake in the room, minus one birthday girl.

Then I feel Iris nudge my leg under the table with her foot. I look at her and see that she's flicking her eyes in the direction of the main pub, through the open double doors.

I gaze through, and at the end of the bar, I can see Gracie smiling and slapping her forehead, talking animatedly with two girls and a guy. They're about her age; maybe a tiny bit older. They're a blur of musty dreadlocks, holey jumpers and piercings. They're some of the new friends she's made from The Den.

They're who she *really* wants to be with instead of us.

I fiddle with the tiny foil-wrapped box that's been lying on my lap.

Inside it is a bracelet with tiny teardrops of a silvery-blue, semi-precious stone dangling from it that I can't remember the name of. All I was thinking when I bought it was that the stone matched the colour of Gracie's eyes.

And all I can think of now is that I'd like to tie this stupid package to one of Dad's helium balloons and let it float off into the sky. . .

Chapter 12

Spaghetti fingers, noodle brain

"Just pretend I'm not here!"

It was tricky to pretend Max's mum wasn't in the room, as she was a) quite a big, tall woman, and b) flapping her son's clean boxer shorts around, taking them from the top of her teetering fresh laundry pile and putting them away in his chest of drawers.

"Mum! Do you *have* to do that now?" Max groaned, stopping mid-beat while we were running through The Beatles' "Here Comes The Sun" together.

At first, Max had wanted us to try some very fast, very loud White Stripes track, but me and Iris had ended up with spaghetti fingers (i.e., in a complete knot) so we ditched that. Next, Iris had suggested Florence and the Machine's "You've Got The Love", but Max had trilled one line in a very funny cartoony voice just to prove there was no way he could sing that high.

And so we were giving "Here Comes The Sun" a go, since it was the song me and Iris had first played to Max, back when we auditioned for him on Monday and thought he was both rude and wrong.

What we were doing together was *starting* to sound OK, but we were all feeling a bit self-conscious, what with the interruptions.

Apart from Max's mum balling up his fresh-scented socks and other unmentionables in front of us, she'd already been in *twice*, first to see if we wanted any juice or biscuits (we didn't) and then again five minutes later just to check we were absolutely *sure* we didn't want juice and biscuits (we definitely didn't).

Then his dad came barging in, asking Max if he'd seen his car keys, and ended up staying for ten minutes, regaling us with tales of Max's drumming history, starting with him banging the TV remote control against his potty when he was sitting on it.

"Was this last year, Mr Willis?" I asked, and immediately regretted it, since Mr Willis went "No, it was when he was two, dear", i.e., he didn't get the joke at *all*. Luckily, Max did and said afterwards that I'd nearly got a drumstick on the back of the head for my cheek.

"Won't be a minute!" his mother beamed now, not in the least bit bothered by her deflated son, who was slumped wearily over his tiny drum kit. (By the way, who knew drum kits came that small? After being in the school orchestra and seeing kits that took up half a stage with glockenspiels and chimes and other assorted percussion gubbins, Max's foldaway electronic drum pads and stands seemed practically *doll*-sized. They sounded pretty good, though.)

"I'll just . . . um. . ." I muttered, taking off my guitar and reckoning the latest interruption meant it was as good a time as any to nip to the loo.

"Toilet, is it, dear?" Max's mum boomed cheerfully. "Last door at the end of the landing!!"

"Thank you," I said, thanking her less for the directions and more for not asking me what I planned to do in there. ("Wee, is it? Or a—")

Closing Max's bedroom door behind me, I felt the tension slip from my shoulders. If I took my time, washed my hands, examined my pores and counted my eyelashes in the mirror, maybe it would give Max's mum a chance to finish the ritual laundry humiliation of her son.

Whatever; I couldn't go back in there too quickly . . . I didn't *dare* catch Iris's eye while the pants flapping was going on. I knew she was on the verge of sniggering as much as *I* was. *And* I knew she was just biding her time, judging when we should talk to Max again about the Rock the Park concert. All we needed was a band name, a few songs, and a singer/drummer who wouldn't vomit onstage with nerves and we could enter. Easy!

Also easy (for real): finding the loo. I'd have come across it without Max's mum's directions, since the house wasn't exactly huge *and* because it had a sign on it that said *Bathroom* in fake, swirly Victorian-style writing (pretty funny in a modern house that was built in the last five years).

I pushed the ornate brass door handle – and walked straight in on Max's big sister Anna, dressed in black leggings and a long pink vest top. Weirdly, she seemed to be sniffing her armpit.

"Oops, sorry!" I mumbled, wondering if the lock was as broken on *this* bathroom door as it was on Iris's.

Spotting Anna's reflection in the mirror, I saw fury

at first, but in the instant it took her to spin around to me, her expression switched – bizarrely – to relief. Or maybe even desperation. Or both.

"God, I thought it was Max. No, please don't go—"

OK, so she'd spotted me trying to back out.

"You're Jenny, right?" she said, her arm still held in the air.

"Jem," I corrected her.

"Yeah. Anyway, I bought these stupid wax strips," she grumbled, pointing to something that looked like a giant bit of Sellotape nestled in her armpit. "But I'm too scared to rip it off. Can you give me a hand?"

Eek. What a strange favour for a virtual stranger. At least I was a stranger to Anna.

"Um, all right," I said, stepping forward and grabbing a corner of the wax strip. "On the count of three. . . One, *two*!"

Rrripp!!

"Argh!" gasped Anna. "You cheated! You stopped at two!"

"A little trick my dad does. Stops you tensing up so much," I grinned, remembering how he used it for the dropping-a-brick-on-a-child's-head gag (it's made of sponge).

Anna managed a weak grin. "OK, I'll be ready for it this time."

With a crinkle and a rustle, she held her other arm up.

"On the count of three," I muttered, grinning as I grabbed the corner of *this* wax strip. "*One!*"

Rrripp!!

"What?!" Anna gasped again. "*More* cheating?"

I gave a *whatever* shrug.

And found her staring at me.

"Hey, do I *know* you from somewhere?" she asked, holding out both her arms to the side to avoid her hairless but sticky armpits gluing together.

"I was here the other day, with my friend Iris. . ." I suggested, trying to remind her of the day she opened the door and gazed at us like we were as welcome as slugs in ice cream.

"Yeah, I know, but it's not that . . . you're just so familiar. . ."

I remembered back to last Saturday morning, spotting my own reflection in the glass by the front door, and surprising myself at the Gracie-ness of my own face. Maybe Anna had glimpsed that too?

"I'm Gracie Wisniewski's sister," I told her. "You were at sixth form with her, weren't you?"

"God, *Gracie*! Yes!" gasped Anna. "Wow, did she ever come back?"

"Nope," I said with a shrug.

"Heard anything about where she is now?"

"Nope," I answered, with another shrug.

"So she only left that one letter when she went?" Anna asked, crossing her arms with a slurpy sort of sticking sound. Her tone was curious, but casual. Maybe some people might have found that a bit heartless, but I liked it. I liked matter-of-fact when it came to Gracie. Sympathy and hugs turned my insides uncomfortably gloopy.

"Just that one letter," I repeated, wondering if Anna knew about Gracie's goodbye note from sixth-form gossip of the time, or from the infamous newspaper article that Max's friend Ben remembered.

"Do you suppose she's still with them? Squatting someplace in another city somewhere? Growing knobbly organic vegetables and saving the world?" Anna laughed wryly.

I felt a slight rush of excitement.

After Gracie had gone, all her other sixth-form friends had drizzled up to our doorstep, shocked and tearful and dumbstruck, as though she'd been run over by a ten-tonne truck, instead of having packed her bags very methodically and jumped of her own free will on to a battered bus along with her buddies from The Den.

It was really great to have someone talk about her as if she was that same annoying person that I knew, and not some saintly missing person.

"Was she different before she went? At college, I mean?" I asked Anna.

Francine and Becci and the others had just sniffled and sighed sadly and said over and over again about how they couldn't believe she'd gone, which hadn't really helped my parents get a handle on how Gracie had been acting outside of the house. (*Inside* the house we knew how much we drove her *mad*.)

"She was pretty cool, most of the time," Anna said reflectively, staring up at the dolphin-patterned shower curtain as she let her memory describe my sister. "But once she started hanging out with those people at The Den and going to all their workshops and stuff . . . *wow*, she turned into a total pain in the—"

She stopped herself, realizing that she might be about to say something completely rude in front of someone who was technically a minor.

"Did you ever go to any of the workshops with her?" I asked.

People in the area had freaked when the old school first got squatted. Letters of concern had poured into the local paper. But the squatters were young and polite and turned the wasteland by the school into allotments and invited the residents of the local retirement home to come and plant with them. Then they started up workshops in tribal drumming and yoga and sculptures-made-from-trash, and held talks on Tibetan healing rituals and South Sea Island relaxation techniques and all sorts of eco *everything* and eventually they became pretty much local celebrities.

From a distance, Mum and Dad thought The Den crew were pretty wild and free and wonderful. They were cool when Gracie and her friends started to go to the occasional art show and workshop and talk there. They *weren't* so cool when Gracie ditched her old friends and skipped her school classes and started hanging out at The Den more and more. . .

"God, yeah! Can't even remember what it was about, apart from the fact that it was b-o-r-i-n-g and Gracie freaked out at us all for giggling!" said Anna.

"Well, who knows; maybe she's running her *own* boring workshops now!"

I smiled, enjoying the image, enjoying the black humour.

"Maybe she's doing one in *Zen Ways To Get Over A Bloke!*" Anna sniggered.

My smile faltered.

"What?" I muttered.

"Well, that's why she went, really, wasn't it?" said Anna, lifting her arms up and down with a slurping noise. "A broken heart. Unrequited love . . . or whatever you want to call it. That's what she hinted at. Never said who, though."

She clocked my dumbstruck expression.

"Oh," she murmured. "Didn't you know?"

"Um, no," I replied, slightly stunned and very, very confused.

"God! Look at the time! Sorry – I've got to go meet a friend but I have to have a shower and get this gunk off. Can you get out now? Ta!"

And with the firm clunk of the door shutting in my face, I found myself back on the landing, with a full bladder and a brain tangled with noodly thoughts.

But before I had a chance to register either troublesome fact, the door flew open again.

"Oops! *I'll* take those," said Anna, grabbing something out of my hands before re-clunking the door shut.

Ah – I hadn't even noticed that up till then I'd still been holding two sticky, hairy sheets of strip wax in my hands.

(Yuck. . .)

Chapter 13

A solitary plink

I was so deep in thought wandering home that I forgot to do my usual swerve on the pavement just outside my house, and so *blam!*, I set off the sensor on the fibreglass snowman.

As the opening bars of "Winter Wonderland" began plonking out, Dad's head suddenly popped up from behind the garden wall.

Spook!

"Hey, Jem!" he called out. "How did your rehearsal go?"

Dad was in his normal-person disguise, looking nearly like a regular father doing the garden on a sunny Sunday teatime. Except he wasn't so much doing the garden as unscrewing the charity box from its spot by the gate (and the average house doesn't tend to have one of those).

"Yep, OK," I told him, as I meandered through the gate.

Dolly was on the path, standing stock-still, staring at the rose bushes. Or quite possibly some bees on them.

"Is it full, then?" I asked, nodding at the box.

"Near enough," said Dad, lifting the box from its stand. "I'll get it counted into bags and then I'll drop the lot off at the children's hospital sometime soon. . ."

"Great," I muttered, bending down to give Dolly a pat.

She gave a small start as I put my hand on her head, and I realized she'd been snoozing on the spot, rather than bee spotting. Then it was *my* turn to give a start, as a small butterfly the colour of the sky suddenly rose up out of the blooming pink rose only centimetres from Dolly's nose.

"Before Gracie left . . . did she have a boyfriend?" I blurted out.

Dad stopped what he was doing and smiled over at me. "That's an out-of-the-blue question!" he said. "What made you think of that?"

"Max the drummer – his sister Anna knew Gracie at college," I began. "I was talking to her this afternoon, and she said something about how Gracie maybe left because of a boy – but she didn't know who."

"Really?" said Dad, dangerously scratching his head with the end of the screwdriver. "Well, that's not what she wrote in her note, obviously. But I suppose your mum and I *did* wonder if she was in love with one of the boys from The Den. I remember the police asking about that."

"Did they?" I asked in suprise. I'd had no idea. But then, I was only eleven when she left and my parents probably didn't tell me every little detail. "Why did they want to know that?"

"Because love is quite a common reason why people run off," Dad continued. "And I guess it did cross our minds that something might have been going on with that Nicko. She mentioned him a lot. . ."

"Yes, but she mentioned the facts and figures he told her about stuff like carbon footprints and Third World debt. She never said he was *cute*!" I replied, thinking that Dad's suggestion didn't quite fit with what Anna had told me. According to her, it sounded more like Gracie was running *from* a boy rather than *to* a boy.

"Well, who knows," said Dad. "Maybe she'll explain more when she comes home. . ."

Warm as it was, I gave a sudden shudder.

The box of chocolates had been sitting unopened on the mantelpiece for a week now, and I hadn't spoken to Mum and Dad about them or Gracie since the day that it happened. They were obviously still talking to each other about her, though. And from Dad's comment, they were still sure that my sister was orbiting Planet Home, ready to re-enter our atmosphere any day now.

With the shudder came a whisper from a dark corner of my mind. "*You KNOW it wasn't because of what she wrote in the note. You KNOW it wasn't because of a boy. You KNOW it was because—*"

Nope, stop there. This was all weird and mad and could drive me seriously crazy. I'd had enough of surprises and spooks and thinking about Gracie for one day.

I had other, non-crazy things to keep me occupied.

"Think I'll go on up and practise a bit before tea," I said, nodding my head backwards towards the case strapped to my back and clonking my head on the neck of my guitar in the process.

"Sure," smiled Dad, as I disappeared under the

plastic deer on the porch roof and into the house.

Dolly followed me stiffly up the stairs, panting as if she were climbing Everest at top speed. Once I got to the landing I turned and waited patiently for her – and heard a noise.

Plink!

It was a small, solitary sound; a little like one note being pressed on a child's toy piano.

Deaf old Dolly heard it too – her small triangular ears went rigidly upright, and as she heaved herself up the last step, she barged past me and waddled straight to the closed door of Gracie's bedroom.

Another shudder. . .

But somehow, having a mad dog in tow made me brave, and I turned the handle of my sister's bedroom door and let it swing open. Before the gap was even wide enough, Dolly nudged her way in, padding over to the dressing table, which she instantly leant against, her eyes blinking drowsily.

Plink!

I expected Dolly to jump at the sound – same as I just had – but she'd fallen instantly asleep. The *plink!* had come from above her, from the top of the dressing table. And the only thing on there that could be responsible was the painted wooden jewellery box. . .

Flipping the tiny silver catch on it, I lifted the lid, and immediately, the plastic ballerina inside began her swirling dance to the tune I'd almost forgotten. How could that happen? It needed to be wound up, didn't it? Had Mum or Dad been in here earlier and turned the key at the back same as I was doing now, just so they could hear the sad, sweet strains of the main theme of *Swan Lake*?

Plink! Plinky-plinky-plink! Plink-plink! Plink-plink! Plink-plinky-plinky-plink!!!

If this whole thing wasn't so weird I'd have laughed, cause something was up with the mechanism and the melody was jangling out-of-tune and way too fast. Elegant real-life ballet dancers would have to flap around madly to keep up with the pace.

But here was something *else* unexpected: there was no jewellery in the jewellery box, I noticed, just Gracie's old, battered iPod, minus headphones (guess she'd taken those with her, along with the iPhone she'd got for her birthday).

I lifted it out and pressed it on, supposing the battery would be long dead by now. But no – like the music box itself, it seemed to have some independent power source and the screen burst into life. I was suddenly keen to sneak a peek at my sister's musical world, and glanced round to see if she'd left her dock and speakers – she had; they were on the shelf above her chest of drawers.

I flipped fast through a succession of tracks, and was amazed to hear that not one of them was R&B, Gracie's favourite music. Well, her *old* favourite music. When had she got into all this slow and bleak stuff? Sixth-form? Or her buddies from The *Den*, more like. Everything sounded miserable, and sort of *folky* (who were Smog, Wilco and Gillian Welch?) with a few oldies I'd heard of in there too (The Smiths and Joy Division – I recognized "Love Will Tear Us Apart", which was great, but *gloomy*).

As I listened to snippets, the ballerina creaked around, and I suddenly realized that the pretty but sad tune sounded faintly like fairground music . . . so it had been the jewellery box that I'd heard in the middle of the night, earlier in the week?!

At the same time as this thought wended its way into my head, a certain scent filled the room.

Not anything evocative like DKNY perfume – just a whiff of silent-but-deadly old-dog fart. The magical moment was gone. . .

Chapter 14

Nurse Jem

"Don't panic – I'll come right now!" Mum sighed into her phone.

So much for her Monday morning off from the café.

We'd walked down the road together to Iris's house, where Mum had planned on drinking coffee at the shiny black marble breakfast bar while she and Viv made plans for the upcoming street party.

Instead, she'd just had a call from one of her staff at the café, who'd told her that Jeff the kids' entertainer had turned up with a bad cold and had only managed to croak his way through two nursery rhymes before his voice gave out. Toddlers were crying, mothers were moaning and bickering, and Mum was needed to come and restore calm in the

Yummy Fun before carnage broke out amongst the cappuccinos and mini-muffins.

"Come by later, Suze!" Viv mouthed, as Mum backed away at the doorstep, shrugging her apologies and listening to the worried voice of the waitress in her ear. "As for you, Jem – go on through to the dining room. The boys are here already!"

The *boys*?!

Well, of course I was expecting Max, whose dad was dropping him around here with his drum kit, just like we'd planned yesterday. (We'd all agreed it might be an idea to rehearse somewhere that *wasn't* Max's house, with all its distractions. Though for his sake, neither me nor Iris mentioned the fact that his flapping boxers had been the main distraction.)

But I hadn't – excuse my fluttery tummy – expected *Ben* to be here too. . .

"Look! That's a tremor, isn't it? I mean, that's *seriously* not good!"

Iris was holding out her left hand flat, and I could see from the dining room doorway that it was shaking ever so slightly.

Max and Ben were standing either side of Iris and staring intently at her afflicted arm.

"You can't play guitar like that!" muttered Max,

agitatedly rubbing his hair into an alarmed furry peak.

"I'd get that checked out, if I were you!" said Ben, his dark brows knitted together in concern.

Poor boys – Iris had really got them (as well as herself) worried.

It was time for Nurse Jem to step in.

"Have you had any breakfast this morning, Iris?" I asked, laying my guitar up against the smoky glass dining table. It wobbled, thanks to one leg being shorter than the others, or the tiles on the floor being laid squint; Iris's parents hadn't quite figured out which it was yet.

"Of course!" exclaimed Iris, sounding puzzled. "Oh, wait! I *meant* to, but then I had a shower and starting watching *4Music* and . . . and I forgot!"

"You've just got hunger shakes. Eat something now," I ordered her, practically handing her a prescription for toast and peanut butter.

"Right! Of course!" Iris nodded, looking well relieved at my diagnosis. "Back in a minute!"

As she disappeared in the direction of the kitchen, Max seemed about to set up his magic folding drum kit, but then he paused. "Where's the loo? Might as well go now. . ."

"Um, down that corridor and right," I told him, shyness curdling in my tummy as the realization hit that I was going to be left alone with Ben.

Maybe Ben felt the same way – he was as quiet as me for a very *loooongggg* second or two after Max had shuffled off.

"Amazing house!" he said finally, gazing around the huge open-plan dining/living area, with its low-slung sofas and glossy high- and low-level tables and chairs.

"Yeah . . . it's pretty special!" I nodded, having a sudden mini-memory of being very small, and sniffing at the wildflowers that used to grow on the patch of wasteground that was here, long before Iris's house was ever thought of. Dolly (younger, smarter, bouncier) was sniffing them with me. Who was looking after us? Mum? Dad? No – I remembered now . . . it was Gracie. In my mind's eye I saw her pointing out the butterflies and the bugs and telling me the names of the flowers. "Dangly-lion!" I'd tried to repeat, and she giggled so much she had tears running down her cheeks. . .

"What's with the half-closed blinds, though?" Ben interrupted my thoughts.

"Don't ask," I smiled wryly, thinking of the broken

remote control, and all the other things Viv and Ray hadn't got round to fixing.

And then it hit me.

We hadn't *warned* him!

"MAX!" I shouted, sprinting past a confused Ben and heading down the corridor that led to the loo. "MAX!! Have you locked yourself in?!"

Stupid question, I realized, looking at the heavy slab of wooden bathroom door that was shut tight. He was in someone's house, having a wee. Of *course* he'd used the lock. But with Iris's lack-of-toast tremors and my Ben-shyness-wobbles, neither of us had thought to trot out the wonky lock lecture that all first-time visitors got in the Fletcher household. . .

"Just coming!" Max called out above the roar of the flush.

No, you're not, I thought, watching as the door handle moved uselessly.

"It jams!" I called out. "Sorry, but you're kind of . . . trapped!!"

"Huh?" Max's voice grunted with a slight hint of alarm on the other side.

"Hold on – I'll get help!"

The next few minutes were a blur of frantic

chatter and useless suggestions, muddled with Viv cursing Ray for never getting around to fixing the many and varied house glitches.

"Jem – use this screwdriver and try to get the handle off, will you?" Viv trilled at me at one point. "Iris – stay on the phone and keep trying to get your dad at his office or on his mobile! Ben – run down to Jem's house and ask her father to come up here with his toolbox."

"Sure, what number do they live at?" I heard Ben ask, as Viv practically pushed him out of the house.

"Oh for goodness' sake, it's the one with Santa on the chimney. Can't miss it," I heard Viv babble, her mind in a pickle of panic. "Hurry! Right, *I'm* going to be in the office trying to find the number of the stupid firm that makes these stupid doors. . ."

And that's when I found myself on my knees outside the bathroom holding a screwdriver that didn't fit the screws, and heard a dull thump from the other side of the door.

"Are you dead?" I asked tentatively.

"I wish I was," came a low-down voice.

I slunk low myself, my cheek on the cool, smooth floor of the corridor.

I'd never noticed before, but the bad design of the expensive, flashy door included a five-centimetre gap at the bottom.

"Hello," I said softly through the gap, spotting a sliver of Max's strawberry-blond tuftiness.

"Oh! Hello!" he replied, turning his head on the tiled floor. I could see his left eye, plus half his nose. Same went for him, except it was my *right* eye, I guess.

"Why do you wish you were dead?" I asked.

"Because it feels incredibly stupid to be stuck in a toilet."

His sliver of face was prawn pink. I guess being held prisoner in a loo *had* to be a pretty terrible experience for a boy with major embarrassment issues.

"Actually, you're stuck in a high-spec, luxury bathroom featuring Italian marble, dual sinks and a spa-style, multi-jet shower, so it's not *that* bad," I said jokily, in an effort to cheer him up.

"You sound like an estate agent!" Max said, grinning (well, *half* grinning, from my perspective), I was pleased to see.

"And you look like a hamster I used to have!"

Oops. There are some things that are better left

thought than said, and that was one of them. Who wants to be compared to a cuddly, furry rodent?

Still, it just goes to show that I really *do* have a remarkable talent – for saying stuff I'll regret. . .

"Did you like it?"

"What?" I bumbled, flustered from my less-than-kind remark.

"Did you like your hamster?" asked Max. He was still grinning.

Phew! It seemed like he might have thought that was a dumbly funny thing to say rather than a wildly rude one.

"Of course! I mean, I *loved* it!" I blurted out, then felt immediately awkward.

Did that somehow sound like I'd told *Max* I loved him cause he reminded me of the hamster that I loved when I was four?!

Arghh!! Why is it so easy to get yourself in trouble with words?

(Uh-oh . . . the box in my head: it had started to open at the mention of trouble and words. But it snapped shut as soon as Max spoke again.)

"We used to have a cat that I hated, cause it scratched me every time I tried to pet it," Max chattered on, luckily oblivious to the stupid things my mouth insisted on saying. "But then it sicked up a furball in my sister Anna's shoe one time, and she put it on – ha! – and I quite liked the cat after that."

"I used to have a sister that I hated." Now what did I go and say *that* for?

"The one that went away?" asked Max.

Uh-oh. So he knew; he must have heard the whole story from Anna or Ben. Help – he didn't want to have some big, long discussion about this, did he?

"Yep," I answered, tight-lipped.

"That must suck," he said simply.

I said nothing back, cause for the first time in ages, I had a lump in my throat and hot spiky tears threatening.

Suddenly, from under the door, a solitary finger waggled my way.

I touched the tip of it with *my* finger.

And for the next couple of minutes, till rescue arrived, the wrong Max and me lay like that.

Two friends, one wonky door and a comforting silence. . .

Ten minutes before the wish

"Gracie!"

I look at my sister – I *know* she's heard Dad calling to her from the van, and I *know* she's ignoring him.

"GRACIE!" Dad shouts louder.

The "Mr Wiggle's World of Giggles" van is stopped at the traffic lights. Dad and Spike are wall-to-wall busy with parties today, so it's a bit of a "spook!" that we've seen them, even if it is just for a second on their way between shows.

Gracie, of course, would rather *not* see them, and would rather that people around didn't think she was in any way connected with them. So she's ignoring Dad, and is carrying on walking very fast in the direction of The Den, where we've got to watch this stupid drumming show she is so desperate to see.

She's not even looking around to check that me and Dolly are behind her.

"*DOOP-DOODLY-OOP-DOOP, DOOP-DOOP!!*"

blasts Dad's horn, still trying to get my sister's attention.

"Go away, leave me alone!" I hear Gracie growl, as I lift my hand and cheerfully wave at Dad and Spike, in their full red-nosed glory.

Spike is biting his lip nervously, obviously aware that Gracie would like him, Dad and the van to be struck by a rogue meteor right now.

But Dad's shameless and unstoppable.

I see him asking Spike to pass him something, and then the lights go green.

He drives alongside us quite slowly, and suddenly puts the thing Spike has given him to his mouth.

"GRACIE WISNIEWSKI – I KNOW YOU CAN HEAR ME!" Dad bellows through the megaphone, making Gracie and half a dozen pedestrians in the road jump out of their skins. "AND I JUST WANT TO THANK YOU AGAIN ON BEHALF OF YOUR MOTHER AND ME FOR LOOKING AFTER YOUR SISTER TODAY!!"

Excellent!

Well, maybe not if you're Gracie and you have zero sense of fun. She stops and turns around to face Dad, and for a moment I think she might be about to shout something at him, but instead she just grabs my elbow and drags me (and I drag Dolly by her lead) through the gates of the old school, under the hippy-ish hand-painted sign that says "All Welcome at The Den!"

Despite the dragging, I manage a quick wave at the van as Dad and Spike speed off, Spike giving me a shy wave of a padded white clown glove in return.

"That was so coo–" I try to say.

"Don't!" says Gracie, in a warning voice, spinning around to glare at me. "Just shut up, say nothing for the next hour, Jem, and we'll get on fine. OK?"

"OK!" I mouth back at her silently and do a zipping mime, which seems to bug her even more.

Wow, my sister is so completely *cosmic*.

By that I mean she's like a big black hole in outer space, ready to suck up and destroy the stars and the sun and anything else that's bright and shiny and wonderful. . .

Chapter 15

Bunny eyes of doom

"It's like they're all *staring* at us."

I could see what Ben meant. The ten white rabbits on the shed wall had been photographed at different angles, but they all seemed to have their beady dark eyes on us. Every picture was in a slightly different gold frame, and under each one, it said "Arnold" with a date of when that particular rabbit happened to be Dad's trusty, furry sidekick.

"That one in particular. . ." he mumbled darkly, nodding at a cuddly white bundle of fluff, as if it had bunny eyes of doom.

Poor Ben – I think my house was creeping him out. Of course, he'd seen the *outside* of it when he'd run down to get Dad and his toolbox on Monday (he came back looking as stunned as if he'd been stuck in a ghost train ride all night).

But today was the first time he'd seen *inside*, and straightaway he'd found it weird the way my strange, very heavy old dog wanted to sit on his Adidas Gazelles. And I guess it was a pity that it was eleven o'clock *exactly* when he came to help me grab some juice and glasses for everyone from the kitchen. When the cuckoos popped out, he hurtled backwards so fast he nearly tripped over the bin.

Also, Ben didn't seem to think it was nearly as much fun as the rest of us to dress up in Dad's dumb stage gear. ("Why?" he'd asked, when Max suggested he try on the purple afro wig. "Why not?" Max had snorted back at him, shoving it on his reluctant head.)

To be honest, I didn't know whether I felt a tiny bit disappointed in Ben's reaction, or a tiny bit embarrassed by my nuts house. Whatever, I suspected he'd've preferred it if we'd carried on rehearsing in the Fletchers' nice, spacious, modern dining room (at least no one would have stuck a purple nylon afro wig on him there).

But after two more days working on our tunes at Iris's, her mum Viv had turfed us out today, so she could have a big street party meeting with a bunch of neighbours. And so instead we were at my place, or in our mega-sized garden shed, to be more exact, which contained no garden implements but an awful *lot* of Dad's props, since it was Mr Wiggle's HQ.

"Y'know, I think I like *that* Arnold best!" said Max, popping up from inside the Punch and Judy box, and pointing (with Mr Punch) at one particular floppy-eared rabbit that I remembered clearly from my childhood.

Even if Ben was a little freaked around the edges, I was pretty sure Max was pleased to be here. For a start, we had a bathroom door that behaved the way a bathroom door was supposed to.

"Me too!" I chipped in, settling my guitar more comfortably on my lap (not easy – I had on the ostrich costume). "I used to dress it in my doll's clothes. I've got an old photo of it in a knitted hat and booties!"

"Aw . . . cute!" muttered Max, coming out from behind the stripy painted box with Judy on the other hand, I noticed. Was he planning on playing drums with both the puppets?

"Can we just get started?" said Iris, sounding quite stern and teacherly, even though she was wearing a pair of monster feet and a bowler hat. "We've got to get these tunes right!"

"OK, OK, boss! What's the rush?" Max said with

a grin, settling himself down at his drum kit and picking up his sticks. (Yes, he *was* going to play wearing Punch and Judy puppets. . .)

"Because we have to be ready for the gig!" I announced without thinking.

Iris shot me a what-did-you-say-that-for? glare. Hadn't we lain on our separate beds in our separate houses last night, watching *Most Haunted* at the same time and talking about this? Hadn't we decided that the best thing to do was rehearse three songs till they were great, and then hope Max would feel confident enough about them to go ahead and take part in the Rock the Park concert?

Yeah, so we'd done all that last night, and now it was Thursday morning and my runaway mouth had to go and *blab*.

"*What* gig?" Max asked, his face as white as any of the bunnies on the wall.

"Rock the Park!" Iris told him straight, tapping on the spook book she had open beside her – the notebook that had the contact number for the concert organizer scribbled in it, as well as guitar parts. Oh, *and* all my random "spooks!", of course.

"What's in there?" asked Ben, reaching down to scoop up the pad.

"Nothing," I said sharply, slapping my hand on top of it. He might sort of *maybe* like me at the moment, but there was a good chance he'd be put off if he caught a glimpse of all the "spook!" ramblings in there.

But uh-oh. . . So much for the sharp voice and the hand slap. Ben was now looking at me like a puppy that had just had its nose tapped for weeing on the carpet.

"Well – we CAN'T do the gig!" Max announced very definitely, completely unaware of any vibes, bad or otherwise, that had just taken place between me and his mate.

"Why not?" asked Ben, who amazingly still seemed more on *our* side than Max's, even though I'd practically snapped his head off. "You've nearly got three songs together!"

Bless Ben and his enthusiasm, he was right. We had "Here Comes The Sun" (just cause me and Iris knew it so well); Green Day's "American Idiot" (cause it was one of Max's favourites), and we'd just started on Michael Jackson's "Beat It" (cause it was another one we knew back-to-front from school orchestra).

"Yeah, but. . ." Max seemed to be flailing about

for excuses, and sounding like me again. "The Rock the Park thing is *way* too big! We need to start with something smaller! Work up to it!"

"It's not Wembley Stadium!" Iris tried to reassure him. "It's just some local bands playing in the local park in front of three dog-walkers and a couple of mums and babies, probably!"

That last bit was a lie, actually. Me and Iris had gone to the Rock the Park event last year, and the grass was packed with lazing crowds, all keen to eat ice cream (from Mum's café) and listen to free music. Still, Max didn't need to hear *that* kind of uncomfortable truth.

"And . . . *and* I don't have a microphone!!"

OK, maybe that – finally – was a relevant point. A singer *did* sort of need to have a mike.

"How much do they cost, then?" asked Ben.

"More than twelve quid, and that's all the money I've got," said Max, looking relieved that he'd come up with something that stumped our idea of performing.

"*I* know!" Iris suddenly announced, getting all our attention. "Jem's dad can magic one up for us!"

A purple, nylon afro came hurtling through the air and hit her in the face.

She was lucky – it could have been one of the puppets, and Mr Punch can *really* pack a punch. . .

"Eighty-nine quid?" I yelped, my shocked breath steaming up the music shop window, staring at the "special offer!" microphone and stand in the window.

"Told you!" Max said smugly.

The four of us had wandered into town together after this morning's fancy-dress rehearsal, minus the monster feet and ostrich suits, thankfully.

"I've got another idea!" said Iris, ignoring the fact that the rest of us immediately groaned. "Ben could be our manager!"

"No *way*!" said Ben. "I wouldn't know how to be a band manager."

"You'd just have to do stuff like persuade the music shop to sponsor us, and give us equipment for free!" grinned Iris.

"Yeah, right!" Ben laughed, rolling his eyes at her as we wandered off towards the shopping centre.

"*And* you can book us lots of gigs, since Max is so keen to do them now!" Iris carried on, teasing two boys for the price of one with that comment.

"Are you kidding?" I butted in. "Did you see some of the useless places Ben put Max's flyers up in? He'd probably get us a gig at the *dry cleaner's*!!"

I was just trying to be funny, and Ben was smiling, but he still managed to look a little hurt. Aargh – I'd thought this morning's awkwardness was over, but I'd somehow managed to say the wrong thing and turn him into a sad puppy *again*. . .

"Or you could be our *roadie*, Ben!" Iris suggested, as we all turned into the square outside the shopping centre. The Thursday morning farmers' market was in full flow and plenty of people were milling around the throng of stalls.

"Yeah! You could carry my drum kit for me!" Max said over his shoulder, joining in the wind-ups as he wended through the crowds ahead of us.

"Nah, I'll carry Jem's plectrum for her!" Ben said back, the tone of his voice making out that he was fooling around, but that shy smile shooting my way telling a different story.

"He really *does* fancy you," Iris muttered in my ear, as soon as Ben turned away.

"Shush!" I hissed, though there was no way that Ben could've heard Iris's whisper above the muddle of chatting shoppers, shouty stall-holders and thud-thud of music coming from somewhere.

"Hey, must be a busker! Maybe we can get

him to join our band if he's any good!" said Max, disappearing through a scrum of mums and buggies and grans with trollies.

Me, Iris and Ben followed, and found ourselves at the edge of a circle of spectators.

"Check it out; it's not a busker after all," said Max. "It's one of those human statues!"

It was actually a robot standing on a box, with a battered CD player on the pavement beside it. Well, not so much an actual robot as someone wearing a boiler suit and a small cardboard box on his head, customized with plastic bottle tops and straws for knobs and antennae, and all of it spray-painted silver. On his feet were silver painted wellies, and on his arms there was some kind of corrugated plastic tubing and thick builders' rubber gloves, all spray-painted silver too.

A couple of little kids were tentatively moving towards the motionless human statue, but before they worked up the courage to chuck a coin in the basket, they squealed and ran back.

"What does the sign say beside the basket?" Max wondered aloud, but none of us could read it clearly because of another kid who was hovering halfway towards the robot, torn between excitement and delicious fear. All I made out was "*Donations go to—*", and that was it.

"What do you think it does?" asked Ben, smiling as the kid suddenly bottled it and ran back to the safety of his mum's arms.

"*I'll* show you. . ." I told him, taking a coin out of my pocket and striding confidently out into the empty circle of paving stones.

I couldn't see the human statue's eyes beyond the slat that had been cut in the box, but I knew the person inside would be watching me.

I chucked the coin in the basket.

Instantly, the corrugated robot arms began to extend outwards, growing longer and longer and stupidly *longer*, making the watching crowds ooh and ahhhh – which turned to *slightly* more alarmed giggles as the giant arms began coming steadily towards me. . .

And then pulled me in for a *huge* robot cuddle.

"You haven't done this in ages!" I said to the silver cardboard head, as the crowds clapped and cheered behind me.

"I have *so* hugged you!" came Dad's muffled voice from inside, as he deliberately misunderstood me.

"Done the human statue thing!" I giggled.

"Well, I had nothing much on today and thought I'd try and top up the donations for the children's hospital! Good idea, huh?"

So that's what the sign by the basket had said.

"*Great* idea!" I answered Dad, suddenly having an *excellent* idea of my own. . .

Chapter 16

Stupid things

In the garden shed, surrounded by Dad's garish props, I'd painted Iris's face.

It was pure white, with tiny, bee-stung red lips and long, drawn-on spidery lashes (I called it cute-clown-meets-geisha).

She'd done me next, decorating my face with a blue butterfly, and adding shimmers of silver glitter along the wingtips ("You keep seeing ones like this all over the place," she'd said, explaining her choice. "Maybe it'll bring you luck!")

We tossed for who'd face paint Max, and *I* lost, so I had to do him (ha!). Anyway, I waffled on about him making a great lion, cause of the colour of his hair and how fuzzy it was, like a mane. (Really, it was cause I was thinking of the cowardly lion from *The Wizard of Oz*.)

And now we were in the intimidatingly grey stone square outside the shopping centre.

Mildly curious passers-by had hovered when they spotted us – two girls and a boy, all dressed in black, with our mismatching painted faces – unpack a tiny drum kit and set an old plastic food tub out in front.

"Jem . . . I can't do this," muttered Max from the side of his mouth.

"You *can*," I hissed back without moving my lips. "Just think of the microphone!"

"No one's coming forward!" Max muttered some more, as he sat ever-so-slightly shaking, with his sticks poised in mid-air.

I squeezed the neck of my guitar, semi-imagining it was Max's neck. He was doing my head in. I mean, this musical human statue act was a surefire way of raising enough money to buy the mike *and* stand that Max needed for us to do gigs, right? And (as Iris pointed out yesterday when we were rehearsing specifically for this) it was a good way of getting used to playing publicly before we did the Rock the Park gig. Wasn't that what Max had said he wanted? To get a few gigs under our belt before we put an entry form in?

"They *will*! It just takes one!!" I mumbled through gritted teeth.

Call me dumb, but I hadn't thought Max would suffer from this much stage fright. I thought he could hide behind the disguise of the face paint and the black clothes, same as he'd hidden behind the tutu and the red nose at the kids' party at the bowling green. But maybe that had worked because his audience was all under *five*. Maybe the mix of knowing teenagers and frowning grannies was too much for him. . .

"And where's Ben?" Max practically squeaked, with his mouth barely moving. "If he was here, he could get things started and chuck us some money!"

At the mention of Ben, I felt that familiar tummy lurch, made worse cause Iris had been trying to convince me that it was only a matter of time before he asked me out. Of course I told her she was wrong, but deep down, I wasn't sure that she was. All I knew was that I couldn't think about it, or I'd never be able to face him, let alone speak to him again. . .

"He's playing a match today, remember?" I hissed.

Ben had promised to get here as soon as his Saturday morning football game was through. But as there was no sign of him yet, we'd just have to hope there was *someone* in the crowd who could kick-start us, same as I'd done for Dad a couple of days ago. He'd come home on Thursday with more than *sixty quid* for the children's hospital. If we got anywhere *near* as much, we'd be well on the way to getting the microphone we needed.

A fairly loud "shush!" came from the other side of the drum kit. I was pretty sure Iris had spotted someone making a move, and tried to use my peripheral vision to locate who it was.

The someone was a lanky, youngish bloke, dressed in a white shirt, red tie, smart grey trousers and shiny black shoes. In that get-up, he looked about as comfortable as a meerkat in a tuxedo.

Mind you, in all the years I'd vaguely known him, he'd looked pretty uncomfortable in his clown get-up too. Maybe Spike Hawkins was just one of those people who never quite fitted in, or fitted in their skin.

"Go for it, Jem!" Spike said now, beaming a goofy smile directly at me, as he tossed a coin in the tub.

Thank goodness for quiet but wonderfully

dependable and lovely Spike. If I hadn't been trying to act like a motionless human statue, I'd have thrown my arms around his neck.

CLUNK!

As soon as the metal dropped on the plastic, what could we do but start up?

"*Doo . . . doo-doo-DOO-doo-doo-doo-doo-DOO-doo. . .*"

It was the music they used on the telly for motor racing, by Fleetwood Mac, who were yet *another* creaky 70s or 80s band that our music teacher Mr Steed loved. But it was perfect for us because we wanted to bash through a tune that a) lots of different age groups of people would know, and b) only lasted for a few seconds.

The plan was that we'd suddenly stop dead, wait for applause, hang on for *more* chucked coins, then launch into another short and furious bit of music. (Apart from the Grand Prix theme tune, we'd rehearsed the intro from Queen's "Another One Bites The Dust" and the beginning bit of *Swan Lake*, which sounded very funny played fast, just like it did in Gracie's wonky-sounding music box.)

The minute it took us to do the tune made my head fizz, it was so exciting. And the clapping, cheering and coin-chucking afterwards felt pretty incredible too.

"That was ace, Jem!" said Spike, shuffling up at the end, by which time me, Max and Iris were still as statues again.

"Thanks," I mumbled through my rigid smile.

"Kind of wished I was doing it with you instead of selling flashy people expensive computers," he grinned lopsidedly as he shoved his hands in his pockets, which made his scrawny shoulders hunch up like there was an upside-down coat hanger in his sensible work shirt.

I realized with a pang that I missed having Spike around as much as he missed performing. It was weird not seeing him slouching in our kitchen on Saturday mornings, waiting patiently for Dad. He might never have said much to me – or to Gracie – but his quiet presence was comforting, a bit like Dolly without the deadly dog farts.

"What does your dad think? He must love it!" said Spike, oblivious to my nostalgic noodlings.

"He . . . um . . . doesn't know," I said softly, feeling a bead of sweat trickle ticklishly down the side of my face.

It felt weird not to have told either of my parents

about this, but me, Iris and Max had decided to say nothing to our mums and dads in case they:

1) freaked out
2) thought it was unethical to get money this way
3) thought we'd look a bit stupid.

("If it's an amazing experience, *then* we'll tell them about it," Iris had suggested yesterday, which made me and Max feel more comfortable with the whole keeping-quiet thing.)

"He doesn't know?" Spike said with an edge of a frown. "Um . . . you *do* know you need a permit from the council to do this, don't you, Jem?"

"Er, no! Do we?" I bumbled, instantly panicked by Spike's words.

Actually, maybe deep down I *had* known there was something a bit dodgy about this, and had avoided mentioning it to Dad in case he pooh-poohed it as a bad idea. The thing was, I just *so* wanted to get the microphone, and just *so* wanted us to be a proper, cool band.

"Uh-huh. Listen, Jem – I'd go now, if I were you," Spike carried on, scrunching his pale eyebrows up to meet each other on his forehead. "The security guys from the shopping centre will give you a really hard time if they catch you, and it might get your dad into trouble. . ."

Sweet, thoughtful Spike didn't have to tell me twice – I stopped being a statue immediately and spun round to see Max already unscrewing his kit and Iris hauling her guitar strap off her back and scrabbling around for her case in the raised flower bed behind her.

If you included setting up and waiting time, our attempts at self-employment had lasted a mighty five-and-a-half minutes.

Something told me that it wasn't quite long enough to raise the funds to buy a microphone and stand.

So much for the blue butterfly bringing us luck. . .

Ben turned up just in time to keep us company as we scrambled away from the shopping centre and any security guards that might have been all set to pounce.

"Good job that guy told you about the permit," he said, rattling along with the plastic money box in his free hand (the other was holding a football).

Iris and I hadn't been able to carry it; we were like packhorses, our guitars on our backs and bits of drum kit in our arms.

"Yeah, Spike's all right," I replied slightly breathlessly, wishing now that I'd tried a bit harder to talk to him over the years. It had suddenly occurred to me that he was probably as shy as Max, and just as much fun underneath, once you burst the bubble of awkwardness. Still, at least I'd always been polite to him. I remembered that all Gracie liked to do was chuck him the odd sarcastic line, as if she was using Spike to hone her sneering skills.

"How much we got, then?" Max asked Ben, as he pushed the main part of his drum kit along the pavement, all neatly packaged up and balanced precariously on his skateboard.

"Hold on, I'll see. . ." mumbled Ben, staring at the smattering of coins in the plastic tub. "Pretty sure it's two pounds and seventy-three pence, plus a Polo!"

"Mint or fruit?" asked Max, looking more like a hamster in that now-smudged make-up than a cowardly lion.

"Mint," answered Ben.

"Chuck it here, then!" said Max, pausing for a second.

Ben expertly pinged it in the air, and Max caught it in his mouth, which was both pretty amazing and very revolting at the same time.

"Yuck!" I groaned, pulling a face at him.

As he shrugged and sucked happily on the coin-flavoured Polo, a memory pinged into my head of Max's comforting finger under the loo door on Monday. Disgusting he may be, but which other boy would think to reach out to a damsel in distress in that way?

And here was another good thing that occurred to me: at least I hadn't thought too much about Gracie since then. The last couple of days there'd been no more music boxes bizarrely twanging out tunes. There'd been no random spooks. There'd been no boxes in my brain creaking open with thoughts that I'd rather leave there, thank you very—

Oh.

I spoke too soon, didn't I?

"Oh, what?" asked Max, frowning at me.

Had I said my "oh" out loud? I hadn't meant to. It was just that I was taken aback to see a) which road we'd just turned into in our hurry, and b) the crane and diggers parked in the weed-strewn playground around the old school/squat.

"What . . . what's going on here?" I said, fumbling for words.

For the last couple of years or so – since Gracie's new friends had been served with the eviction notice by the new owners of the site and left – the entrance to the old once-squatted school had been locked with a chain that had eventually rusted over. But today the chain was gone, and both the ornate gates were swung wide open, to let in the crane and diggers, presumably.

"It's finally getting knocked down. There was a big thing about it in the local paper the other day," Ben explained. "They're going to build flats here instead, I think."

It shouldn't have mattered to me one little bit. I should have been glad to see the whole thing go, with its memories of stupid crusties doing stupid drumming workshops and taking stupid sisters with them when they stupidly packed up and went.

(But more than all that – if I was honest – I wanted *not* to think about stupid things that stupid *me* said once upon a time. . .)

"Jem?" I heard Iris ask me. "Are you OK?"

She knew I'd be thinking about Gracie.

"Uh. . ." I muttered uselessly, as I remembered the

last time I went through these gates. On the way in, I was being dragged by my sister, and on the way out, I was running to catch her up as she stormed off home, Gracie seething with dark, unknowable thoughts and me flitting between rage and regret.

"Y'know, I never went to The Den," said Ben. "Some of my friends did, for the art classes or karate classes or whatever. But my mum didn't let me. She thought the people there were all. . ."

"Weird?" Max suggested.

"Uh, no – *smelly*!" Ben grinned. "It didn't matter how well they fixed the building up or turned the gardens into allotments or whatever, Mum couldn't figure out *how* they could stay clean in a squat with no running water or electricity!"

They *had* fixed up the building well, I remembered. There were those stunningly patterned Indian throws pinned up at the windows and a gorgeous, cosy glow of candles on the long winter evenings.

"I came here a few times to some of the kids' drumming workshops," Max surprised me by saying.

"Did you?" asked Ben, sounding surprised too. "I never knew. But then we didn't know each other till secondary school, I guess."

"My dad took me," Max explained some more. "I remember he spent his whole time staring at the teacher guy's blond dreadlocks!!"

"That was Nicko," I mumbled, remembering the last time I'd seen him, at the drumming show – the one I reluctantly went to with Gracie. The one I wished I'd never gone to, so things didn't turn out the way they did.

(*Shut the box, Jem!* I warned myself.)

"Yep! *That* was him!" nodded Max. "How did you know?"

"He was friends with my sister."

I felt uncomfortable talking about it, and Max seemed uncomfortable having accidentally brought the subject up.

"Oh, yeah . . . course. Hey, listen; anyone fancy noseying in the window?" he blustered pinkly. "See what it looks like in there?"

"Definitely!" said Ben, and before I knew it, the boys were unloading the drums and football just inside the gate and were stomping off across rubble and weeds towards the building.

"Someone will see us!" I warned them, scanning around for workmen, who might chase us off even *more* grumpily than shopping centre security men.

"They won't see us at *this* end of the school – we're out of sight!" said Iris, carelessly dumping her load alongside the boys' gear and following them over. "Come on, Jem!"

She waved me to join them, an encouraging smile on her cute-clown-meets-geisha face.

I hesitated for a second – then gave in to my own curiosity.

As I dumped my own guitar down and stepped through the undergrowth towards the others, a pale blue butterfly fluttered out of the tangled grasses somewhere between me and Iris.

We both looked at it, then each other, then burst out with "Spook!"

The boys whirled round.

"Hey, what's with the spook thing?" Max asked, him and Ben both intrigued.

Me and Iris, neither of us answered straightaway, probably because we both knew that they were boys; normal boys who liked football and *Guitar Hero* and probably laughed at fart jokes. The thing was, *so* far, these normal boys seemed to like us and we pretty much liked them. But would Max and Ben think we were really *lame* for being hooked on random bizarre happenings?

"We just . . . erm . . . think coincidences are kind of fun, and we always say 'spook!' when they happen," Iris eventually stepped in to explain.

"Yeah, but so what happened there? What were you spooking about?" said Max.

"We saw a butterfly. A blue one. We keep seeing the same ones over and over again – at least *Jem* does!"

Now the boys turned from Iris to me, expecting more. But what was I supposed to say? Wouldn't they think I was beyond *nuts* if I told them about all the small strangenesses that had been going on lately?

My brain decided it would be a bad move to say anything.

But clearly my mouth had *different* ideas. . .

"All this . . . well . . . totally *bizarre* stuff's been happening in the last couple of weeks," I blurted.

"Yeah? What sort of bizarre stuff?" asked Max, while Ben just frowned at me.

Urgh . . . I really shouldn't have started this. Here was someone very cute who might just *possibly* have a crush on little old me, and by the time I tried to explain all the Gracie coincidences, Ben would be halfway out of the gates with his football under his arm, never to be seen again.

And Max: coincidences had led me to him, *and* his sister Anna. If I told him that, he'd be clattering off into the sunset with his drum kit before you could say "I'm not crazy, or a witch, honest!"

"It's . . . it's nothing," I muttered.

"It's her sister," Iris jumped in. "It's like all these mad things are completely linked to her! We've been writing them down. Look, I'll show you!"

"No, don't," I mumbled, grabbing her arm to stop her running back for her notebook.

Iris stopped, realizing it was a step too far. But the boys were still staring intently, and weren't going to let it go, I didn't suppose.

"Look, I know it sounds insane, but since my mum's birthday, things have gone a bit weird," I waffled. "My sister left a present on the doorstep – which is the first time we've had contact for more than two years – and after that. . ."

I trailed off, not sure how to continue. Unfortunately, because *I'd* just spoken, Iris immediately seemed to think it was OK to start up again too. And by start up, I mean blab just about *everything*, no matter how loopy it sounded.

"Yes, but that part isn't what's bizarre, though,

is it?" Iris jumped in, sounding flustered for some reason. "Get this – Jem's been hearing Gracie's music box playing! When there's no one in the room, and no one winding it up or anything!!"

(*Please stop!* I wished silently to myself. *You're making out like I'm deranged, Iris!*)

"And the butterflies she keeps seeing; they're *just* like the ones painted on Gracie's music box! Can you believe it?"

(*No, they probably can't*, I thought, wanting to curl up and die.)

"And *then* there's the fact that Jem's dog Dolly keeps turning up in Gracie's room when the door's always kept closed, and Dolly can *hardly* open doors with her paws being all arthriticky, can she?"

OK, so I wanted to point out that having arthritis or not wasn't *really* the point when it came to paws and opening doors. But that didn't bother me as much as Iris making the coincidences sound completely *pathetic*.

Hardly head-swirling cosmic amazingness at all – just the useless ramblings of a couple of childish *dingbats*.

I mean, what must Max and Ben *think*?!

"Cool!" they muttered simultaneously.

(Spook!)

"So, uh, what do you think the bizarre stuff all *means*, Jem?" asked Ben.

I walked past him and stood on my tiptoes, looking through the window. It wasn't that I was ignoring his question; I was just giving myself time to answer. As I frantically mulled over a non-loopy reply, I realized I was peering in on the old school hall, where all the Den workshops and art shows and musical performances had happened.

It was empty now of the drums and the rugs and floor cushions that were once here, of course, but the walls were still a riot of colour, every inch of them covered in technicolour murals of twining flowers and beautiful faces, rainforest animals and mystical symbols.

"It probably doesn't mean anything," I said vaguely, deciding that "vague" was the *least* mad way to explain things.

Without instantly responding, the others joined me, stretching up alongside to gaze into the hall.

"Or it *might* mean that your sister's trying to get a message to you, like *psychically* or something!" suggested Max.

Ha!

At least that made me laugh.

"Gracie was the *least* psychic person you ever met!" I tried to tell him, thinking of the endless pamphlets and printed downloads she had on every environmental campaign going on in the known universe, the ones she'd take in to share with her politically enlightened eco-warrior buddies at The Den. "Horoscopes and hauntings and . . . and *coincidences* – she thought *all* of that was just superstitious rubbish!"

"Yeah, but *you* don't," said Max softly, turning his hamster face towards me.

Bling! Bling! Bling! my phone rang suddenly.

Mum's number came up on the screen.

"Hi, Mum!" I answered, feeling a rush of sudden guilt.

Was that because I was *here*, trespassing? Or because I was keeping a secret from her? (About performing outside the shopping centre just now? Or cause of the *other* secret that kept trying to slither out of the box in my head. . .)

"Hey, Jem! Look, I need your help," said Mum. "It's just—"

I was only half-listening to what she said.

That's cause I found myself leaning my still blue, glittery forehead against the windowpane, staring in at a section of the mural.

The face I'd just zoned in on amongst the stylized blossoms was absolutely *beautiful*. Her hair was long and tumbling like tendrils. Her eyes were slanted, cat-like. Her expression was still and serene.

The face belonged to Gracie. . .

Chapter 17

Memory failure

"Hey Jem, maybe they're poisonous spider bites!" gasped Iris, sitting on Gracie's bed and holding up her legs so she could study her spotty ankles better. "Should I go to the doctor, just to check?"

"I told you – it's nettle rash," I said, chucking her the cream I'd just dug out of the bathroom cabinet. "We were standing knee-high in the stuff at the old school just now, remember?"

"Mmm," mumbled Iris, as if she was reluctantly accepting my more realistic and less dramatic diagnosis.

"So what are you doing in here anyway?" I asked, since I'd left her in *my* room two minutes ago.

"Just wanted to look at Gracie's things again, after seeing her on the wall today," Iris said dreamily, forgetting about her spotty ankles and the cream, and getting up to waft around the room, as if she was trying to sense the essence of my sister (Eau de Grump, if it came in a perfume bottle).

I gave in and joined her, grabbing hold of the music box and flumping down cross-legged on the bed. I'd started stressing out less about being in Gracie's room lately. Specially when me and Iris had got back today and found we had the house to ourselves (Mum was still at the café, and Dad was out clowning somewhere).

"You know, if someone painted *me* like that, I think *I'd* be sort of in love with them," Iris said, pulling open the wardrobe door. "Probably enough to run away with them!"

"Hurumphhh!" snorted Dolly, who was leaning up against the door.

I couldn't have put it better myself.

"Yeah, but Gracie *didn't* leave because she was all *chuffed* that someone had painted her face in some mad mural on a squat wall!" I replied, remembering how Ben had spotted Nicko's name scrawled underneath Gracie's face.

"OK, OK, so she didn't say so in the note she left," my best friend mumbled, rifling through the clothes still hanging uselessly in the wardrobe.

"No, she didn't!" I said, opening the box and pinging the plastic ballerina back and forth on its tiny spring. The bracelet with silvery stones that I'd bought her for her birthday . . . it wasn't in here, *or* on the stand where she kept her bracelets and necklaces.

What happened to it? I wondered. *Did it end up in a charity shop, like most of the things she cleared out of her room and her life. . .?*

"Yeah, but maybe she left the being-in-love bit out?" Iris suggested.

"Why would she do that?" I said back, stopping with the pinging in case I broke something in Gracie's room, i.e., committed a cardinal sin. "Gracie *always* said what she thought."

(Yeah, and what she thought was usually along the lines of: "I love the planet"; "I *hate* my ridiculous surname that I always have to spell!"; "I love the environment"; "I *hate* that none of you understand me!"; "I love hanging out at The Den"; "I *hate* this family!")

"Maybe she wanted to keep her secret love *secret*. . ." Iris joked, slapping the back of one hand to her forehead, like some old-time silent movie actress.

"And maybe you've got it all back to front," I replied. "Max's sister Anna said it was 'unrequited love', remember? You don't *run off* with someone who doesn't love you back, do you?"

"Whatever," Iris said with a shrug, carrying on with her clothes rummage. "Great spooks, though, weren't they? The butterfly and Gracie's face on the wall I mean?!"

"Mmm," I muttered, watching the ballerina twirl and feeling kind of washed out with the drama of the day, all of a sudden.

To be honest, I quite fancied a break from all the secrets and spooks. I didn't even have the energy for Iris and her hypochondria. I flopped back on the bed and pulled the pillow over my head. I wished I could block everything out for a while and sleep, but there was no chance of that. Mainly because it was still only quarter to twelve.

And because Dolly was snoring.

And because Iris wasn't going to shut up any time soon.

"I mean, *this* . . . how could she seriously leave home without *this*?" I heard her say.

I flipped the pillow back off my face and stuck it under my head with a sigh. I saw that

Iris was holding up a nicely distressed, double-breasted khaki jacket with dull brass buttons and epaulettes.

"The thing is," I replied, "I think when you're planning to run away from home, you take the *important* things with you like your phone and your bank card, and your birth certificate and passport and stuff. I don't suppose you worry *too* much about whether or not you've got a cutting edge jacket in your rucksack!"

"Oo-OOO-ooo!!" Iris raised her eyebrows at my jokey sarcasm before ducking from the pillow I'd just chucked at her.

"Lame joke!" I told her, suddenly grabbing the pillow and chucking it at her.

"Missed!" she said brightly. "Anyway, try the jacket on, Jem – it'd really suit you!"

Hanging out in Gracie's room, lying on her bed, flipping open her music box, looking through her stuff; I'd relaxed enough to do all that. But trying on her clothes? My knee-jerk reaction was that it was a big, fat nope-I'd-better-not.

"Nah, I don't really like it," I lied.

"Chicken!" Iris teased me, but she knew not to push it, and hung the jacket back up. "Hey, Jem,

I was just thinking about what Max said earlier. . . D'you think that Gracie really *is* trying to get a message to you or something, with all the spooks that keep happening?"

I suddenly worried that me and Iris had watched *way* too many TV programmes about telepathy and assorted otherworldliness over the years. Maybe (like Gracie would say) coincidences were just something you should shrug off. It might be better than what was happening now; i.e., I was starting to feel *more* than a little freaked out.

"Iris, you *know* Gracie was never into that kind of stuff, so it doesn't seem likely, does it?" I replied, trying to sound rational and unfreaked. "And secondly, if she *was* going to be sending out psychic vibes, why would she send them to *me*, and not Mum, who's desperate to hear from her, probably any way she can? Remember, Gracie couldn't *stand* me!"

"She liked you *some*times!" said Iris, flopping down on the bed beside me and making Dolly snuffle in her sleep with the wobble of it all.

"Oh, yeah? Name a time when she liked me!" I dared her.

"When you gave her *that*," Iris said blithely,

tapping her finger on the box in my hands.

"This?!" I said in confusion, staring down at the ballerina. "*I* didn't give her this! I think she got it from Granny or someone!"

"Uh-uh!" Iris contradicted me, with a shake of her head. "Just after our house was built and we moved in, it was Gracie's birthday. I remember it cause it was only the second time I'd been invited round here to play. And you'd bought her *that*."

"Did I?" I muttered, turning the box in my hands and staring at the blue butterflies as if that would help me remember. But I was only seven back then, and while loads of my childhood memories were sharp as pins (my first time on a trampoline; falling over and cutting my knee in the playground; seeing a dead jellyfish on holiday; the day Dolly got lost in the park), I couldn't remember giving this to Gracie.

How embarrassing that once again, Iris's memories of my sister were clearer than my own murky ones.

"She must have been. . ." Iris did a quick calculation. "Fourteen? Anyway, I guess she had to have liked the box – and *you* – at the time. Enough for her to hang on to it for years. And she never hung on to anything much, did she?"

I didn't know what spooked me more – seeing Gracie's face staring at me from a wall today or knowing that once upon a time, my sister actually *liked* me. . .

A different wish

I'm cross.

"It's NOT FAIR!"

"Don't be silly, Jemima," Mummy is saying, but I'm not looking at her.

My head is on the glass of the fish tank and it is nice and cool but I still feel all hot and bothered inside.

"Is NOT!" I sniffle.

"But *Dolly* is your pet!" Mummy says.

"Is not – she's *Gracie's* pet!"

Gracie got Dolly when Mummy got me. I *know* that is a true thing. And I know that I am very, *very* cross.

I love that hamster and he loves me and I want to have him. He is very sad and lonely in that hutch and he needs to leave the pet shop and come and live in my bedroom where I will feed him seeds and apples and let him share my crisps when I am allowed any.

"And there's Arnold too!" Mummy is talking on and on. "You can play with him any time, you know that!"

"He is *daddy's* magic pet! That doesn't count!!"

I stamp my foot to show Mummy just how cross I am and how unfair everything is.

My head hurts with grumpiness.

And I do not like the little lobster thing that is sucking up old food and bits of fish poo in this tank. It has a mouth like a hoover and googly eyes that are staring at me.

I would not like it as a pet.

"Jemima, darling, come on – it's time to go home," says Mummy.

But I'm not going anywhere.

Not without my hamster who has the cutest face and fat cheeks and *ooooooh*, I want to cuddle him and squeeze him and love him for ever and ever until he dies.

"I just WISH I had a pet!" I moan.

My eyes and nose are both very drippy and I have a pain now in my throat and my chest. It is a very, very sad pain.

"Hey, Jem!"

That is Gracie's voice but I am not going to turn round because she will just say I am silly and tell me we need to leave right now too.

"Gracie!"

Mummy says Gracie's name in a surprised voice. I sort of wonder what Gracie has done but I'm not going to look round so there. Maybe she has knocked over the tub full of dog crunchies. I did that when I was three and it made a big mess and I cried.

But I am four now and don't do silly things like that any more.

"It's OK – I bought it with my pocket money!" I hear Gracie say.

What did she buy?

"Gracie, that's very sweet, but what about a cage and everything?"

What did Gracie buy that needs a cage???

"Oh, I hadn't thought about that bit!"

Gracie just spoke with that laugh she has in her voice sometimes. I like that laugh. Maybe I WILL look round.

"See, Jem? I made your wish come true!"

Gracie is kneeling down to me with a big smile on her face and a fluffy hamster in her hands.

Oh, I LOVE my big sister more than sweets and monkey bars and anything in the whole wide world!

Except maybe hamsters. . .

Chapter 18

Punk it up!

"The face painting's fantastic! What made you think of doing that?"

It was a busy Tuesday morning in the packed Yummy Fun café, and I was squirming a bit at Mum's question. Max and Iris were being jumped on by too many toddlers to squirm – or even hear what Mum was saying.

"Um, it's just something we were playing around with," I replied, missing out the part about the shopping centre disaster on Saturday morning.

The thing was, I'd painted us all to look like hamsters, since I reckoned that would pretty much appeal to our audience of mostly under-threes. Plus I was *good* at painting hamster faces (the evidence: Max's so-called "lion" look when we were human statue buskers).

"Well, thanks a million for stepping in while Jeff's off sick. I didn't want the children disappointed again!"

There'd practically been a riot on Saturday morning, when Jeff and his laryngitis meant there was a café full of sobbing, roaring children demanding "Twinkle Twinkle Little Star" and a bubble machine. Jeff had been told by his doctor to rest his non-existent voice for a week, which was why Mum had thought about asking me, Iris and Max to step in. So all day yesterday, we'd been in my garden shed, rehearsing nursery rhymes (rock 'n' roll!).

"It's fine, Mum. We're looking forward to it. As long as the kids don't *break* Max before we've even started," I said, wondering what the mothers were doing while their offspring seemed to be using Max as a climbing wall.

"Oh, dear, yes!" said Mum, just noticing the mayhem with an indulgent smile. "Come on, boys and girls! Can we have everyone sitting down nicely on the floor, please!"

At Mum's words and gentle clapping-to-attention, the assorted toddlers didn't exactly *sit*, but at least they backed off and hovered, which was an improvement.

I took a couple of steps forward, and gave Max a wink. He gave me a cross-eyed look in return. Good; he seemed nervous-but-excited rather than nervous-and-about-to-be-sick.

"Mums and dads; grandparents and childminders; boys and girls!" Mum chirped to the room.

And Ben too, I thought, smiling to myself as I saw him sitting on a pink plastic chair between a harassed bloke bouncing a bawling baby on his lap and a breastfeeding mother. Ben looked as out of place as a grape at a steamroller convention.

"Can I present to you . . . The Hamsters!!"

No – it wasn't the *actual* name we'd settled on for the band (we still hadn't a clue about that), but it would do for today. *And* Thursday, if we didn't mess up and Mum asked us back to fill Jeff's spot again.

"One, two, three, four. . ." Max counted out, tapping time on his drumsticks, launching us into our first number, which happened to be that rock classic "Humpty Dumpty".

We played it OK.

Max sang it pretty well, I thought (only slightly wobbly for the first few notes).

The reaction we got was amazing.

Amazingly *bad*.

The song came to an end, and instead of applause, all we heard was the buzz of indifferent chatting. I shot a look over Max's head at Iris, who gave me a tiny face twitch back that translated – under the face paint – as "Help!"

I glanced down at Max, expecting to see a trembly human jelly. But hurray, he was already tapping his drumsticks and counting us into "Sing A Song Of Sixpence", even if he *was* cringing inside.

Again, the grown-ups blanked us and carried on with their conversations, as if we were some wallpaper music trilling from the radio.

Meanwhile the little kids just sat sucking their teddies' ears or hitting their organic juice cartons off each other's heads.

Ben seemed to have his eyes on me the whole time (which was almost as unnerving as the complete lack of interest from our captive audience). As we clattered the song to an uncomfortable halt, he came bounding over, stepping over an assault course of toddlers to get to me.

"Do it like you did for the human statue act!" he told me hurriedly.

It took a second for what he meant to sink in.

I turned to the questioning faces of Iris and Max, who hadn't been able to make out what Ben had said above the baby babble.

"Punk it up!" I ordered them.

Like the good friends they were, they clicked straightaway. Fast; we were going to play it very, very *fast*!

"One-two-three-FOUR!" yelped Max at high speed, and we walloped headlong into a manic version of "Wee Willie Winkie", followed by a wild "Hickory Dickory Dock" and half a dozen more nursery rhymes done at breakneck speed.

For the first few seconds, the children and the parents watched open-mouthed (with drool, in the case of some of the littler members of the audience). Then the kids suddenly began bouncing like Tiggers that had been fed on a diet of pure sherbet.

And result! The adults were clapping and whooping along, covering the wails of the odd baby with non-punk tastes in music.

"Thank you very much! See you on Thursday!!" said Max, leaping up from behind the drum kit at the end of our set, holding his sticks aloft. "Er, if that's all right, Mrs Wisniewski!"

"Of course it's all right!" said Mum, coming

towards us through the clapping, stomping crowd. "That was fantastic! Really, really fun! Now if you want to grab your instruments before the kids dismantle them, you can come on and grab some cake and drinks. Oh, and your fee, of course!"

"Fee?" said me, Max and Iris all at once (spook!).

"Well, yes!" Mum laughed at us. "You didn't think I expected you to do this for free, did you? I pay Jeff thirty pounds a session, so you'll get the same!"

I looked at Iris, the same thoughts crossing our minds. Not just the fact that after this week we could afford – by chucking in all our spare cash too – the microphone and stand, *but* as a band we now knew the three of us could sound good together AND we'd played a few small warm-up "gigs", in the shape of the human statue experiment and this one today at Mum's café.

So Max had no reason not to play the Rock the Park concert any more, did he?

"S'cuse me!" Iris smirked at Max as she wriggled her phone out of her pocket and glanced over at the poster with the rainbow, right behind Mum's counter. "Got a call to make!"

"Yeah, you've run out of excuses, Max Willis!" I told him gleefully.

As the truth clunked into Max's furry head, I saw his jaw drop.

He might as well have had the word "GULP!!" hanging over his head in giant cartoon lettering.

"But hey," said Ben, who we hadn't even noticed stepping over small children again to join us. "If you're going to try and get on the bill for the concert, aren't you forgetting something?"

As soon as he said it, we all got it.

"A name!" yelped me, Max and Iris, as a trio.

Of course, Iris and I immediately grinned and "spook!"ed in tandem.

And in the noisy lull that followed that, we all knew – surrounded by kids, crumbs and the confusion – that we'd just decided what to call ourselves. . .

Chapter 19

Stage fright and splats

We had a name (The Spooks!).

We had our microphone (Max went and bought it after our rehearsal yesterday).

We had our slot at the Rock the Park concert (right now; we were the second band on after the Brownies recorder troupe, and before the granddad jazz band).

We had our musical style (we planned on bamboozling the audience by doing slow songs *fast*, inspired by our punked nursery rhymes).

And we had about thirty seconds till we were due on (with only one member ready to perform – *me*).

"What took you so long?" I hissed at Max, as he hurried passed the triumphant Brownies and other milling bands loitering on the grass behind the stage.

Max shrugged; I guess he didn't need to explain that stage fright had made him rush to the backstage Portaloos as the clock tick-tocked towards our performance. He'd probably be blushing right now, but you couldn't tell under all the white face paint.

In my role as hair and make-up artist for the band, I'd ditched the hamster look for today, and went for pasty pale white on our faces to suit the new band name, plus we were all wearing white T-shirts and either black leggings or jeans. But weirdly, the spook-look just seemed to accentuate Max's chunkiness and tufty gold hair. He looked more like a hamster than *ever*.

"By the way, Iris is coming – I just saw her getting served," Max told me, throwing a thumb back over his shoulder.

"Aargh!" I roared quietly, in case my voice could be picked up onstage and transmitted to the couple of hundred people lazing on picnic blankets out front. Which of course included all our parents – and Ben.

"But Iris *had* to get some water – she's suffering from dehydration, remember!" Max tried to reason.

"She is *not* suffering from dehydration!" I insisted, knowing my best friend's powers of hypochondria all too well. "She's only a bit thirsty – she had two packets of ready-salted crisps at the café before we came over here!"

I pulled at my jacket collar – well, *Gracie's* jacket collar – in irritation, wondering why I'd bothered to fret about what to wear (OK, *steal* from my sister's room) if this gig wasn't going to happen. . .

"It's all right!" I heard Iris's voice suddenly call out. "I'm here, I'm ready!"

I gritted my teeth and stomped up the three wooden stairs to the stage without looking at her. Normally, I *always* indulged Iris's imaginary aches, pains and ailments, but today I didn't have the patience. The compere bloke was about to announce our name any sec—

"And put your hands together for The Spooks!, everyone!!!" bellowed the guy onstage.

I heard a small squeak coming from behind me, and knew without looking who'd made *that* noise.

"Don't worry – we can do it!" I turned and said to Max, above the sounds of whoops and clapping.

"There are too many people!" Max winced, staring at the floor as he walked towards his drum kit.

"Cross your eyes, then!" I ordered him. "That way they'll just look like blurry blobs!"

I really, really hoped my advice was going to work. Cause being onstage is like finding yourself at the top of a rollercoaster, knowing there's nothing you can do to stop yourself from thundering to the bottom. Freezing like a statue was all very well when we were doing our busking thing in the square beside the shopping centre, but it wasn't an option now.

"One-two-three-*four*!" I was relieved to hear Max count us in, and immediately we went hammering into a lightning-speed version of the sad song "Yesterday" by The Beatles; another of the more bearable tunes that me and Iris had learned for the school orchestra.

As we played, I spotted Dad in the crowd without any problem (since he'd come here straight from a party in his clown gear), and saw Mum waving frantically too (which was ace, as the next song we were doing was one of her favourites: "Everybody Hurts" by REM). Right next to them were Viv and Ray, giving us the thumbs up.

At the end of that first number, they and the rest of the crowd went nuts. Maybe it was because we were quite good, or maybe it was because everyone was just blown away by the sight of three teenagers with a weird look and a cross-eyed singing drummer.

But who cared? It felt *good.*

Barely pausing (so nerves couldn't trip him up, I suppose) Max launched us into "Everybody Hurts".

And now I could see Ben – hanging out with Max's parents and sister Anna – nodding his head and grinning up at us.

Well, *me*, actually.

Just me.

Wow, that was a mighty strange flipping sensation in my stomach. Thundering out my chords, I shuffled round slightly in the hope of catching Iris's eye, to see if I could psychically zap her a distress call ("Help! I'm thrilled but embarrassed!! Eeek!!!").

No chance; she was having *far* too good a time, doing mini-pogo jumps around the stage in time to the music, all buoyed up by the fact that some of the audience were now on their feet, dancing and clapping along.

There was no sign of any "dehydration" now – Iris was a whirling, girl-shaped ball of energy, a beam of a grin on her face as she jumped this way and that and—

And fell backwards off the stage with a twang of her guitar and a dull thud. . .

The receptionist at the Woods Hill Children's Hospital probably saw a lot of strange sights – kids who'd got their heads stuck in buckets, or wedged marbles up their nose, for example – and she was obviously trained to react in a calm and professional manner, whatever the circumstances.

"Can I help you?" she smiled serenely at a clown, a human albino hamster and an extra from a horror movie (I could see my reflection in the glass cabinet behind her head – crying had left streaks in my white make-up that made my face seem like it was *melting*).

"Our friend's daughter came in a little while ago with a suspected broken leg," said Dad, sounding serious, despite the painted red grin. "Her name's Iris Fletcher."

"Ah, yes – she and her parents are being seen right now. Do you want to take a seat?"

"Yes, thanks," Dad replied. "But in the meantime, we've got a donation here for the hospital. . ."

Dad turned to a distracted Max, who gave a startled "Oh!" and then stepped forward to place the tartan shortbread tin on the reception desk.

"Um, that's kind of you. . ." the woman said, still smiling, but clearly wondering why a clown, hamster and horror-movie extra wanted to give her some biscuits.

"It's just over two hundred pounds," I said quickly, yanking the lid of the tin to display a haul of coins.

On the way over here in the Wiggle van, Dad had remembered that he'd left the tin in the back, ready to drop off at the hospital whenever he had a spare moment – or a medical emergency, I guess.

"Ah, *right*!" murmured the receptionist, sounding genuinely warm now. "That's fantastic! Really wonderful! Let me call someone to come and collect it and put it somewhere safe. . ."

Our job done, we wandered over to the waiting area, where Dad and I flopped down on two of the blue plastic chairs.

Still feeling antsy, Max stayed on his feet, idly examining the framed, blobby bits of artwork crowding the walls, all done by former (very young) patients, by the look of the wording underneath them.

"All right now, Jem?" Dad asked, wrapping an

arm around me.

"Yeah – it was just a bit of a shock at the time," I said, remembering the panic I'd felt when I rushed to the edge of the stage, not sure what I'd see. (What I'd seen was a stunned Iris lying flat on the ground. She'd burst into tears as soon as she saw my face, which started *me* off, of course.)

"Yeah, but it was one of your 'spooks!', though, wasn't it, Jem?" said Max, grinning over his shoulder at us.

"What's that, then?" asked Dad, uncertain what Max was on about.

"Iris fell off *exactly* when I sang the line '*everybody hurts*'!" Max laughed.

"Pfffff!" I sniggered snottily, caught out by Max's black humour.

Dad was chuckling too.

"Poor Iris!" he said, giving my shoulder a cheery squeeze. "But hey, what was your last song going to have been?"

"Joy Division's 'Love Will Tear Us Apart'," I told him, sniffing.

"Wow – that's *another* old one! I didn't know you knew it! What made you think of that track?"

I hesitated, not sure if I wanted to tell him I'd

been rummaging in Gracie's room, listening to my sister's gloomy songs on her iPod. (Neither he or Mum seemed to have noticed that I was wearing her jacket. Why oh why had I taken it? The band's bad luck was probably Fate's way of kicking me in the back of the knees for helping myself to something of my sister's.)

"Um, just heard it around," I said vaguely, rummaging in the jacket pockets in search of a potential tissue for my dribbly nose. Nothing there . . . so I tried the small inside pocket, which was bulging slightly.

But instead of feeling any long-crumpled lumps of soft paper, my fingers wrapped around what felt like a twined, soft *something*.

"Well, at least you'll have it all ready to perform for our street party," Dad said positively.

"When's that again?" asked Max in a slightly nervous-sounding voice, pausing as he noseyed at the paintings.

"Next Saturday. Oh – I guess I should let Jem's mum know what's happening," said Dad, suddenly glancing up at a sign on the wall showing a mobile with a red line through it. Scooping his phone out of his multicoloured trouser pocket, he walked through the nearby automatic doors to make his call.

And now I was going to check out the something in Gracie's jacket . . . it was one of those plaited, brown leather wristbands that some of the boys at school were into wearing.

There was a tiny white label tied to it. A price tag, I thought, till I turned it over and saw – in neat, spidery writing – the words *From Gracie xxx*.

My heart lurched.

Who was this present for?

And why had whoever-it-was never received it?

"Hey, Jem . . . have you seen—? Hey, *that's* cool! Is it for me? Gee, *thanks*!" I heard Max say, switching from some unfinished question to a general bit of cheekiness.

"No it's not," I said hurriedly, stuffing the wristband back where I'd found it. I'd show it to Iris later, and see what she had to say. "Spook!", probably, since I'd no sooner mentioned one of my sister's favourite sad love songs to Dad than I came across an unsent boy present in her pocket. . .

At that very thought, I felt myself slump down in my seat, now completely exhausted by the overload of "spook!"s, never mind the stress of Iris's unexpected stage-dive.

I've had enough of weirdness! I said to myself, closing my eyes and making a wish.

I wished for life to go back to normal (however normal it could get in my family).

I wished that I could do simple, straightforward stuff, like hang out with my best friend, play in a band, take my dog for waddles around the park, and think how I felt about a boy called Ben liking a girl like me.

Without being distracted and interrupted by coincidences.

I had really, really, *really* had enough of them.

"Uh, Jem; I was just going to say, the kid who drew this one. . ." Max carried on, pointing at a small sign under a felt-tipped pen picture of a stick-girl and a rainbow. "It says *Gracie Wisniewski*, *aged 4*. Is that the same Gracie as, er, *your* Gracie?"

At any other time – like when my best friend hadn't been injured and I wasn't dumbstruck by having yet *another* coincidence come up and slap me in the face – I might have got my sarky head on and said, "Yeah, like there're *so* many Gracie Wisniewskis out there!"

But since my best friend *had* been injured and I *had* been slapped in the face by yet another coincidence, AND I didn't know that Gracie had ever had a picture on display in here, I just shut up, plain and simple, since I didn't know what to say about *anything* any more.

"Yes, that's her!" Dad answered Max, arriving back after his quickie call with a broad smile that practically matched the painted-on one. "Gracie was in and out of this hospital all the time when she was young. She had to get check-ups because she was born with a hole in her heart."

I knew *that*, of course, even if I didn't know about the picture. But Gracie's illness had happened long before I was born, so the fact of a poorly Gracie was like some bedtime story I vaguely remembered, same as tales of Dad touring around Europe being a busking magician and Mum serving coffee and apple doughnuts in a Swiss café with a cuckoo clock during her gap year.

"The doctors hoped the hole would close up by itself," Dad continued, "but when Gracie was four, they decided she'd better come in for a operation to fix it for good. And that's when she drew *this*."

"Is that why you like to donate money to this place?" said Max, figuring it out.

"Absolutely!" Dad beamed some more.

OK, so Max had asked his question, and now I found I had one of my own. One that had never occurred to me before.

"Dad . . . did you and Mum ever worry that she might die?"

It came out horribly bluntly, but I really wanted to know. I'd never properly thought of what my family had been through in that long ago time before me.

"Oh, yes – quite often," Dad admitted, his smile(s) fading at the memory. "In fact, you know something, Jem? Your mum and I made ourselves a bit of a promise once . . . we said that *if* Gracie was all right, we wouldn't ask for anything more. We wouldn't be pushy parents who pressured her to do exams or get a good job or all that stuff. We'd just be glad to have her, and let her be who she wanted to be."

And what she wanted was to be away from us, I didn't say, though I suddenly understood why Mum and Dad were sad but not angry that my sister had gone. . .

Flunk!!

A sudden clunk and flap of opening doors made us all whip round automatically.

"Hey, check *me* out!" said Iris, spotting us straightaway.

I was pleased to see my best friend smiling again, though I wasn't entirely sure why, since it was now pretty clear that she had *definitely* broken her leg.

"Can you do wheelies in that thing?" Max joked, bursting the bubble of seriousness.

Iris stuck her tongue out as her dad manoeuvred her closer to us in her wheelchair.

"It's just to get her out to the car," Viv explained, holding up a pair of crutches. "*These'll* be how she gets around for the next few weeks!"

"Yes, but everyone's missing the point," said Iris, pointing to her raised-up leg. "Isn't it beautiful? They let me choose and it was really difficult – they had *so* many excellent colours! What do you think, Jem?"

I looked at the mauve cast and thought, *Well, that's going to be a pretty interesting rock star look at the street party gig next week!*

"Hmm . . . I think it needs glitter. And maybe some ribbon round the top," I said instead, moving round to take the chair's handles from Ray.

If my friend finally, *honestly* had something wrong with her, I was going to be the best nurse ever (i.e., one that *wasn't* borderline sarcastic). . .

The day after the wish

"Are you OK? You feel cold. Do you want a jumper? I can get you one. Or a hot drink?" says Iris, being the best nurse ever, checking that I'm all right, with her arm around me in case I fall apart.

"I'm OK," I lie, wondering if I'll ever feel OK again.

It's been six hours since Mum found Gracie's note.

It's been five hours and fifty-nine minutes since Mum first tried to ring Gracie. (No answer. No ringing tone, to be precise.)

It's been five and a half hours since Dad finished calling around all her friends (the old ones, that is).

It's been just under four hours since Viv and Ray and Iris shipped up here, to keep us all company and make endless cups of tea.

It's been three and three-quarter hours since Mum phoned the staff at the café and asked them to run the place on their own today.

It's been two and a half hours since Spike came

round to collect the clown-and-magic gear so he could do this afternoon's kids' party on his own (he looked so white and shaken when he left that I wasn't sure the painted-on smile would be enough to hide his shell-shock from the children).

It's been an hour and a half since Mum found the old SIM card and phone shop receipt in the bin in Gracie's room, and figured my cunning sister had swapped her number so we can't get in touch.

It's been fifteen minutes since the nice police officer left. She'd listened very sympathetically but said that as Gracie was eighteen and had written a very specific note that seemed to suggest she wasn't in danger or vulnerable, there wasn't terribly much the police could do. (She'd also handed Dad a bunch of leaflets about missing persons helplines and said she'd check in on us from time to time.)

And it'll be a few moments till the receptionist at the local newspaper puts Mum through to the main reporter's desk, I guess.

In the meantime, she has her hand over the receiver and is having a scrambled semi-argument with Dad.

"Why does your mum want to phone the paper?" whispers Iris, her ears straining to hear the tense words coming from out in the hall. (I'd rather blank them out.)

We're curled up on the sofa with Arnold and each other, pretending to watch Saturday-morning telly, but neither of us could probably tell you what the presenters had just said, or what band played about five minutes ago. I'm feeling so numb that it's not occurred to me to stop Dolly from chewing on the magic wand Dad must have left lying about somewhere.

"Mum thinks it would be good publicity – if anyone sees Gracie around or knows where the crowd from The Den have moved on to, they can call the newspaper and let them know about it," I tell her.

"And why does your dad *not* want your mum to call the paper?"

"Because of what Gracie said in her note, I s'pose."

"Can I see it? The note, I mean?" Iris whispers, as if it's some top secret document.

Though if Mum gets her way, it probably won't stay secret for long. I can guess what it'll be like if she *does* do an interview with a reporter – they'll want a picture of me and my parents hugging and looking sad, and they'll want Mum or maybe me to hold a photo of Gracie (the studio portrait of us both is the most recent). Then they'll ask to print the goodbye note.

I understand that Mum wants to try every possible way to track Gracie down, but I get Dad's point. If

Gracie is still somewhere in the area and sees herself and her private letter displayed for the whole wide nosy world to pore over, she'll go nuts. There's no better way to make certain she *never* comes back.

"Sure," I say, hauling myself up off the sofa and grabbing it from the shelf, where Mum put it when she was seeing the police officer to the door.

I hand it to Iris. I don't need to read it again; Gracie hasn't written much, and her not-much is pretty much embedded in my head.

Dear Mum and Dad –

Don't freak out, but my friends at The Den are moving on and I've decided to go with them.

You're going to flip, I know, but they didn't make me – I want to go.

The bottom line is, they care about what I believe in, and I fit with them, the way I don't fit in at home.

Don't stress – I've got everything I need and I'll get in touch somewhere down the line. But right now, I can't say if that'll be next week or next month or next year.

You've got to just trust me and let me do this.

Gracie

No love, no kisses, no mention of me. (No wonder.)

"Dolly, *drop* it!" I *order*, realizing I should do *something* useful, even if it is just rescuing a bit of plastic. *Anything* to push my dark, guilty secret from my mind.

Picking up Dad's wand – which is chewed, bent and covered with drool – I wave it uselessly around, wishing oh-so-hard that I could magic away the wish I made yesterday. . .

Chapter 20

Hide & secrets

The last few days had been great.

OK, if you didn't count the fact that Iris had broken her leg, of course.

The reason the last few days had been great was because – since Iris's major splat at the weekend – there'd been a grand total of *zero* coincidences and spook! stuff.

Maybe it was all over.

Maybe the wish I'd made in the hospital waiting area – for boring, ordinary normality – had come true. (Oh please, oh please, oh *please*. . .)

Most of the nice, boring, ordinary days this week had been spent in the garden shed rehearsing for this Saturday's street party. We'd been running through some new sad songs to do fast, since Iris had announced, "I never want to hear that REM track again!" from the comfort of a stool first thing on Monday.

Sometimes Ben had been there listening, and sometimes he hadn't.

Sometimes he watched Iris or Max as they worked on their parts (wearing stupid costumes from Dad's collection, in Max's case) but most of the time Ben, er, watched *me*.

Sometimes I managed to carry on as if I didn't notice he was doing it, and sometimes my tummy flip-flopped and my fingers tripped over the chords I was supposed to be playing. . .

Max and Iris (and Ben?) were coming around again this afternoon, but this morning I was going to have a lazy time, starting with sofa surfing and a magazine. I had it tucked under my arm (my magazine, not the sofa), and was looking forward to being horizontal any second now.

"It's been three weeks since this came," I heard Mum murmur, *just* before I walked into the living room. "I really thought it meant she might. . ."

I stayed where I was, bare feet on the wooden floor of the hall, and peered in.

Mum was running her finger around the edge of the star-shaped gift tag attached to the box of chocolates on the mantelpiece. Dad had his arm draped around her, and was giving her shoulder a pat with his padded white clown glove.

"I know, Suze," he was saying softly. "I know. But I guess she'll come when she's ready."

If I was a lovely daughter – one *without* unspoken guilt and a secret inside a box in my head – I might have gone and joined in the group hug.

As it was, I silently backed away . . . then nearly jumped out of my skin as the cuckoos in the kitchen burst into song. But at least I was able to use their next nine tweets to cover the sound of my feet padding upstairs at high speed.

At the top of the landing – parked outside Gracie's room – was the laundry basket.

Parked *inside* Gracie's room – the door wide open – was an old, doddery dog, chewing on something it shouldn't be chewing on.

"Dolly! What's that?" I hissed at her.

Uh-oh – I'd just spotted what it was. A twined leather wristband.

"Give it here. Drop it!"

Where had she found that? I'd put it back in the pocket of Gracie's green jacket. . . But then I *was* kind of distracted on Sunday evening when we'd got in from the hospital. My memory was of yanking the jacket off quickly and stuffing it in the wardrobe. Maybe the wristband had fallen out? Rolled under the bed? Only to become a dog chew toy at the earliest opportunity?

"Yew," I mumbled, patting Dolly's head with one hand and holding the drool-covered band in the fingers of the other. Whoever had been meant to get this present wouldn't exactly want it *now*.

I glanced round – there was a box of tissues by the jewellery box. I grabbed one out and gave the band a rough rub, then wondered where to put it. Back in the pocket of the jacket? Or why not in the jewellery box, since there was nothing stored in there at the moment, now that I'd left the iPod wedged in its dock?

I flipped the pretty latch and lifted the lid.

Plink!

The ballerina moved around one notch. Where she stopped looked odd, as if her elegantly outstretched plastic arm was pointing to a corner of the lid.

Oh.

She was "pointing" at a ruffle of satin lining that had come loose. . . I picked at it with my nail, and it pulled away, along with the mirror that the ballerina could watch herself dancing in.

Oh again.

There was a *note*!

For a second, I held my breath, as I yanked the thin, folded paper from its hiding place. I knew without a doubt that I shouldn't read it – but I also knew that there wasn't the faintest chance that I wouldn't.

I flopped down on the edge of the bed, and Dolly flopped her head on my knee, as if she planned on scanning the contents too.

The note began. . .

"*Ha-whoooooooo-OO-ooo!*"

"Sorry," said the security guard at the shop entrance, "we don't allow dogs in here."

"Yeah, I know," I replied, hovering by the doors, as some ambient dance track drifted out of hidden speakers and set Dolly off on a yodel. "I just need to have a quick word with that guy *there*. . ."

The security guard looked where I was pointing, hesitated a moment, then figured I could be a teenager with a hefty allowance and a desire to spend it on an expensive gadget – dog or no dog.

"Sure. Wait there and I'll get him to come over to you."

"Thanks!" I said, wrapping my hand around Dolly's lead. It wasn't so much that I needed to stop her running off – a snail could trot faster than Dolly these days – it was more that I needed to cover up the fact that my hand was shaking. The other one, the one holding the note, was trembling too.

And now here he was, walking towards me, smiling questioningly.

All the way over here, I'd rehearsed different ways of saying what I had to say, but now it came to it, I'd gone blank. After an awkward second or two, I decided to simply start the same way the note had.

"Hello, Spike!"

"Hey, Jem!" Spike answered, leaning over and ruffling Dolly's ears affectionately. "What's up?"

"I . . . uh . . . I found something that was meant for you," I mumbled, handing over the now-crumpled piece of paper. "It was in Gracie's stuff. I don't know why she didn't give it to you."

Spike suddenly went a luminous shade of pink, and his own hands seemed to be shaking as he took and unfolded the note.

I watched as his eyes quickly scanned the words. The words that I knew off by heart, same as the other note that Gracie had left behind.

Hello, Spike.

I know you did what you thought was right, but I think you're so wrong.

You didn't give us a chance.

And using my dad as a reason is the worst. It's like you chose him over me.

You chose a stupid red nose over my heart!!

Goodbye for good.

Gracie

Spike read it at least three times; I could tell from the way his eyes kept jumping to the top of the page and down again.

Spike.

Goofy Spike Hawkins, who was always sitting in our kitchen, drinking tea in a dumb clown costume, waiting for Dad to be ready. Sweet, shy Spike, who'd politely answer Mum's questions about school and then university, and who'd rub Dolly under the chin as she sat on his shoes. Kind, laid-back Spike, who'd always have a hi for me, even though I was just a kid, and who'd take the scathing looks and sarky remarks from Gracie as she bustled around the kitchen whenever he was there. And she was *always* there when he was, now I thought about it!

Wow – I'd always thought Gracie couldn't *bear* him. "Too busy getting buckets of water in the face to get a *proper* job, Spike?", "Tripped up any kids in those clown shoes and made them cry?" she'd say, as she tossed her long hair in the face of his stuttered responses.

All those endless, barbed remarks; they'd just been *her* way of getting Spike's attention, same as boys at primary school when they thump you and bug you because they like you and don't know how else to show it. So much for Gracie being older and wiser!

"We, um, we went out a couple of times before she left home," said Spike, before adding, "*She* asked *me*!"

He said that as if he wanted to add "Can you believe it?", but I guess I could. Even if it had taken me till recently to realize it, he was a gentle, genuine guy.

"And I liked her, of course," he continued. "I mean, she was *gorgeous*, but *way* too. . ."

Poor Spike didn't owe me any explanation, but I really appreciated that he wanted to give me one, so I decided to help out.

"Serious? Grouchy? Sarcastic?" I suggested.

Spike gave a relieved laugh, realizing that he wasn't about to offend me with any unfair adjectives when describing my big sister.

"Yeah, well . . . that's pretty much it. And she *hated* me working for your dad. She thought the clown stuff was *so* naff."

"I know," I shrugged, vaguely aware of a tugging of the lead. Automatically I loosened my grip slightly so Dolly could amuse herself by padding about for a sniff around our feet.

"The thing is, I loved working for Mr W – I had a blast the last few years!" said Spike. "And at the time, I didn't want to get another job – mine was loads more fun than stuff my mates at school were doing, like stacking shelves in Tesco or whatever. So cause of that and all the. . ."

"Seriousness, grouchiness and sarcasm," I helped him out again when he hesitated.

"Right, that!" he said with a shy smile. "Cause of all that, I decided to sort of . . . *end* it. And I said it was because it was too weird dating the boss's daughter. I knew she was upset, but not that she was *this* upset."

He held the note up . . . and then, as if he didn't know what to do with it, he went to hand it back to me.

"No, it's all right – it's yours. Oh, and so's this," I told him, passing over the slightly mangled wristband. "I'm pretty certain this was supposed to be for you. Though I don't know why she didn't give you this either."

"Um, right. Thanks," Spike muttered awkwardly.

I turned to leave, but it was trickier than it sounded; Dolly had settled herself for one of her nano-sleeps against a two-metre-high cardboard display replica of a Nokia phone.

"Come on, baby," I said, as I nudged her awake and attempted to gently drag her towards the shopping centre exit.

"Hey, Jem!" I heard Spike call after me. "I – I've always felt it was my fault, y'know? I mean, I never told your dad about me and Gracie, and – and I always thought it was maybe because of *me* that she left. . ."

Poor Spike – he'd been keeping that burden of a secret all this time? No wonder he'd looked so shattered that morning we discovered she'd gone. I thought he'd been wobbly about doing the kids' birthday party on his own, but instead he'd been knocked sideways by worry and guilt.

"Don't worry! You really *weren't* the reason she

went!" I called back to him, feeling my own guilt well up inside again.

I could say what I said to Spike with certainty, because it was becoming more and more obvious to me that the reason Gracie disappeared from us was locked inside the box in my head.

Oh yes, I knew *exactly* what had made my sister go. . .

Chapter 21

The Best Friend Radar failure

The street party was in full swing, and someone had murder in mind.

"I could kill him!"

Those non-community-minded words were said by an elegant woman, draped in swathes of floaty fabrics, accessorized by jangly bracelets and a coin belt.

As she spoke, she continued painting an intricate black henna tattoo on the hand of a slightly giggly seventy-year-old lady called June, from number 73.

"Why do you want to kill him?" I asked my in-disguise mum.

"Your dad promised Viv *ages* ago he'd definitely organize the licence we needed for the street party, and you know what he just told me?"

"Let me guess. . ." I muttered. "He forgot?"

"He forgot," Mum said with a nod. "He said that without Spike, he was totally taken up with organizing the parties, and he didn't remember to do it. Let's just hope no one official turns up today to check up on us!"

"They won't *now*, Mum," I said reassuringly, looking at my watch and realizing it was early evening already. Where had the time gone? It had been mayhem in the morning, helping Dad and Ray dismantle all our reams and reams of fairy lights, so that they could be strewn over and around the stage.

Then this afternoon had whizzed by in a whirlwind of races, along with the tombola, tug of war, Cutest Pet Competition, talent show and other assorted dumb-but-fun events.

"Anyway, never mind me moaning," Mum said cheerfully, as she finished off her tattoo with a flourish. "Are you having fun, Jem?"

"Uh, yeah. . ." I answered hesitantly, as I spotted a small girl skipping down the road with what looked like a blood-soaked nail in her cheek.

Oh, dear.

"Hey, hi, Kitty!" I said, stopping her in her tracks. "The big girls at the face-painting stall – what did you ask them to do on your face?"

"A ladybird! Is it pretty?"

"It's a bit smudged," I said, smearing away the painted-on nail with my finger. "Go back and ask them to do it again – better! Say Jem says so!!"

Me, Max and Iris were all due to go onstage any minute, or I wouldn't have handed over my make-up brushes to a couple of untrustworthy ten-year-old neighbours.

"Speaking of your dad, I haven't seen him for a bit," said Mum. "Have you spotted him?"

"He was teaching Max how to do balloon animals about ten minutes ago," I told her.

"Really? And how was that going?"

"All right . . . though Max's looked like balloon *slugs*. Don't think they were going down too well with the kids – but I could be wrong," I said, as (spook!) a toddler passed by in his mother's arms, happily wafting around a white balloon that looked a little bit like a giant maggot.

But where was Max now? And Iris? Though Iris had an excuse – she couldn't go anywhere very fast on her crutches.

"Actually, I'd better find the others," I said distractedly to Mum, wondering quite *how* I was going to do that, since the street was heaving with people.

A-ha – the stage! It was all set up with instruments, but there was no one up there at the moment, unless you counted our singing snowman, reindeer and Santa Claus. They'd been transplanted from ours earlier and draped in hula skirts, Hawaiian shirts and flowery leis, to get them in the summery mood.

Holding on to my guitar with one hand, I scrambled up and gazed around.

"Jem!!" a voice called up, and I found myself staring down at Max and Iris (in their spook-white make-up) and Ben (blush). "What are you doing? Going solo?!"

"I was looking for *you*!" I grinned at Max. "Where've you been?"

"Me and Ben were rescuing her crutches," he replied, tilting his head towards Iris. "Two boys had nicked them and were pretending they were light sabres!"

"Ah! You're my heroes!" I joked, then spotted Ben's face light up. The fact that four throwaway words from me had made him so *instantly* chuffed set off that familiar flipping sensation in my tummy.

"*Burp!!* Oops, sorry!" said Max, interrupting my awkward moment. "Shouldn't have had that last burger. . ."

"Yeah, three was probably enough!" I teased him, as he helped Iris hobble up the stairs at the side of the stage and guided her over to a waiting stool.

But I was secretly pleased – if Max was in the mood to eat (too much), it meant his stomach wasn't clenched tight with excess stage fright.

"Hey, Jem – can you wrap this around my stool for me?" Iris asked, taking something out of the pocket of her guitar case.

Pale purple tinsel; she was coordinating the stool with her plaster cast!

"Sure," I nodded, taking the long, sparkly decoration and a roll of sticky tape from her.

I was just winding it round the stool legs when I heard Viv's voice.

"Listen, everyone; the sun's starting to set, so I'm going to ask someone to crank up the generator and get all these lovely lights on," she called up from the front of the stage, with Ben hovering close by, in prime fan position. "Then I'll come and introduce you. OK?"

"OK," the three of us said in unison (spook!).

"By the way, Jem!" Viv added, just as I'd started to turn away. "You're looking gorgeous today – you're the spitting image of your sister in that outfit, did you know that?!"

That outfit; she meant Gracie's stolen jacket, of course.

"Um, no," I answered her, flummoxed, and getting my fingers knotted in the sticky tape.

From my kneeling position, I glanced up at Iris.

"Your mum's just saying that because she's seen Gracie wearing this *way* back, only she can't remember," I whispered to my best friend.

"No – you really *do* look like her," Iris answered, with a voice that suddenly sounded strangely wobbly.

"Are you all right?" I asked, straightening up. Was Iris nervous? Or did her leg hurt, maybe?

"Jem, can I tell you something?" she said urgently.

Face-to-white-face, Iris looked *more* than wobbly – she looked completely *panicked*. Uh-oh; she wasn't about to announce she had gastroenteritis or legionnaire's disease and that we'd have to abandon the gig, was she?

"I did something really, *really* stupid. . ."

"Yeah, you fell off a stage last Sunday, remember?" Max laughed, as he settled himself behind his kit.

"Max!" I said to shush him.

I felt bad; I knew Max was nervous and just fooling around, but then again, I'd never seen Iris looking so stressed, not even the time she accidentally dropped her phone down the loo in Year Seven.

And something was definitely wrong with my Best Friend Radar – bizarrely, I just couldn't tune in to what was stressing her.

"What? What did you do?" I tried to encourage her.

Iris bit her lip, to stop it wobbling perhaps.

"I've been meaning to tell you for *ages*. . ." Iris said, clutching her guitar to her chest, like it might give her some protection.

"Tell me *what*?" I asked her, trying to keep an edge of alarm from creeping into my voice. I knew Viv would be expecting to introduce us *any* second.

"Well, I – I mean, you know the present on the doorstep?"

"The chocolates? From Gracie?" I said. We'd eaten them – finally – today. Mum had shared them round Dad, me, Iris, her parents, and Max and Ben once all the Christmas decorations had been taken down and reinvented as a stage-set. ("As good a time as any!" Mum had beamed, though I knew it meant a lot to her to give away her precious gift.)

"The thing is . . . well . . . the thing is, Jem . . . *I* did it. *I* put the box there."

The expression on my face must have read "????"

"Look, I *know* it's nuts, but when I did it, I had this stupid idea that it would cheer your mum up!" Iris burbled, her words tumbling out in a guilty rush.

"What?" I gasped, not knowing quite what to say or how to react.

"Well, it was cause you'd all been round at my house the night before, and my mum had said something about how much Suzanne must miss Gracie at a time like her birthday, remember?" she rattled on. "And I *love* your mum, Jem. Suzanne's great, isn't she, Max?"

Iris glanced around at our friend, who nodded madly, like a very confused hamster holding drumsticks.

"And so the next morning," Iris continued, "I bought the chocolates and printed out a gift tag and I, uh . . . I left them on your doorstep."

She took a deep breath.

"The thing is, Jem, I realized it was a really, *really* idiotic idea about five seconds after I did it."

My heart was thundering with shock. How could my so-called best friend – who was practically part of the family – do something so infuriatingly, thoughtlessly STUPID? I mean, didn't she realize how much she'd raised Mum and Dad's hopes?! It might have been meant for the right reasons, but anyone with a *brain* could figure out it was just, well, *cruel*.

But what about me? I muttered silently to myself, as the box in my head tumbled over, spilling stuff out.

"You're mad at me, aren't you?" said Iris, tears welling in her eyes. "I've been feeling so, *so* guilty and I've wanted to tell you *all* this time, but—"

"I *am* mad at you," I interrupted flatly. "But it's not as bad as what *I* did."

Iris's jaw dropped.

"What did *you* do, Jem?" asked Max, coming out from behind his drum kit to stand beside me. What must people in the street have thought? That we were having a very earnest chat, arguing about a last-minute change to our set list, maybe? If only. . .

"What did you do, Jem?" Iris repeated softly, putting her hand on top of mine.

"*I'm* the reason Gracie went. I made a wish, and next thing she was gone."

There.

It was out of the box, out of my head and out of my mouth at last.

"What are you on about, Jem? Are you saying you're a *witch*?" Max asked, fooling around and trying to make me smile, I think. (In the circumstances, he had *zero* chance of that happening.)

"It's totally my fault!" I said, feeling hot and cold shivers rush through me. "I was with her the day before she left – she was babysitting me and dragged me to this awful drumming show at The Den."

"I remember that," Iris muttered.

"She started moaning on and on about me and Mum and Dad. She was about to say what she *always* said; stuff about wishing she wasn't part of our family, and wishing she could get away from us . . . and I said – I said—"

My chest felt like it had an elephant sitting on it. It was only Max gently rubbing my back that made the pressure ease and the words carry on.

"I said I wished she *would* go. I said I was fed up hearing her always threaten to leave and that nothing was stopping her and we wouldn't miss her and . . . and that I *hated* her."

There; that was all of it.

The whole toxic lot.

I was the reason my sister left. Not Spike Hawkins, or Mum or Dad – little old *me*.

Max and Iris stared wordlessly, as the blah-blah-blah of the hubbubing crowd rumbled all around us. Another time, that background sound would've got me giggling, but not today, not right now, when I was spilling my horrible secret.

"You're joking, right?" said Max, finally.

He was grinning!!

Huh?

I turned automatically to Iris. What was this? My best mate was frowning at me, like there was something she wasn't *getting*.

Had they both heard right? Was I talking in English, or had the stress fried my brain and made me blab my innermost turmoil in Cantonese, maybe?

"Why would I be joking, Max?!"

"Cause that's just *dumb*, Jem!" he told me in no uncertain terms. "I mean, *that's* not a proper wish! And your sister's not going to have taken off just cause you were a bit *rude* to her! Me and Anna say MUCH worse stuff to each other all the time! I mean, only last night she was swearing her head off and calling me a—"

"EVENING, EVERYONE!" Viv suddenly boomed through a microphone, as the reams of lights and the snowman and co. pinged into brightness all around us. "ARE WE HAVING FUN SO FAR?"

No, I thought, my feelings in free fall.

I couldn't make sense of what Max had just said, but Iris obviously agreed with him; she'd been nodding her head off just now.

Could it be true that Gracie *didn't* leave because of what I said? But I'd lived with that guilty awfulness for the last two and a half years. . .

"WELL, LET'S CARRY *ON* WITH THE FUN! NEXT, I'D LIKE TO INTRODUCE TO YOU A FANTASTIC NEW BAND," Viv boomed out to the eagerly waiting throng. "FROM OUR VERY OWN STREET, I GIVE YOU JEM AND IRIS WITH THEIR FRIEND MAX. MAY I PRESENT . . . THE *SPOOKS*!"

Whooping and cheering: *always* a good start. Only it wasn't *Max* who was frozen with fear this time – it was *me*.

"Jem? What's up?" I heard him hiss at me as he hurried back behind his drum kit.

"I can't remember how it starts!" I mumbled back,

making my mouth as still and motionless as it had been when we were human statue buskers.

The new set we'd been practising all week; the sad-pop-songs-done fast, starting with Christina Aguilera's "Beautiful" . . . right at this very twisty-headed second I couldn't figure out how on *earth* my fingers were supposed to move on the frets to make that happen.

"Let's do an old one, then!" Max hissed some more. "'Love Will Tear Us Apart'?"

He glanced from me to Iris on her stool and back again, and Iris nodded as soon as she saw me do the same.

"A one-two-three-four!!"

SLAM! On Max's cue, we thundered into Gracie's favourite track at top speed and on automatic pilot (well, *me* anyway).

But as I thrashed out the familiar chords and stared out over the smiling audience, a strange thought occurred to me.

What if . . . what if I'd got a lot of things back to front, and inside out?

I mean, was Gracie actually as *bad* as I pictured her?

If I was honest, my memory of her wasn't *always*

that reliable; after all, it was *Iris* and not *me* who remembered the *With Loveness*, *Gracie xxx* message in that old Mother's Day card (yes, the one Iris obviously copied on to the gift tag!).

FLASH! Suddenly, some long-forgotten, random fuzzy images zipped into my mind. . .

A girl who put her arm around me in holiday snaps.

A girl who loved the corny, twee, hand-painted jewellery box I presented her with.

A girl who took me and Dolly for walks in the days before Dolly was deranged and I was annoying.

A girl who bought me my very own pet with her pocket money when she was eleven and could've been spending it on lipgloss or CDs instead.

A girl who taught me the difference between buttercups and dangly-lions. . .

I shook my head, scared I was going to concentrate on the slide show in my head instead of the track I was supposed to be playing. But *still* more thoughts slid right in.

If cold, spiky Gracie could sometimes be nice, what about *me*?

I guess laid-back Jem could blast off as much as

Gracie used to do (I *did* snap at the baseball-cap morons when they laughed at me in Dad's van; *and* at Ben under the birthday party table; *and* at Max for fooling around just now).

And the sarcastic sense of humour . . . I had that too (just ask Max, since he was often at the receiving end of it, and Ben, who looked like a wounded puppy whenever I turned it on him).

Wow.

Gracie and me; we were more alike than I'd ever realized!

Which was deeply worrying. Or immensely great. I was just too confused and rattled to figure out which at the moment.

Better just concentrate and play, I ordered myself, staring over the tops of the heads of the audience, who seemed in the fading evening light to be just one dancing blur . . . *apart* from the woman at the back.

Perhaps she was different because she was standing still.

And no one else was wearing what looked from here to be a smart suit.

Or holding a clipboard.

Arghhhh!

She was the dreaded someone from the council,

come to check on our non-existent licence, all ready to shut our street party down!

Frantically, I scanned the crowds for Mum or Dad, or even Viv or Ray to let them know. . .

"JEM!" I heard Max suddenly yell into his microphone, instead of the words to the song.

I flipped round, ready to frown at him. What was he up to?

But he wasn't looking at me – he was pointing up, up at the reams of coloured bulbs directly above my head that were flickering ominously and making a high-pitched hissing sound.

BANG!!

In one short, shocking second the lights blew, the smell of something rubber burning filled my nostrils, and a surprisingly heavy cable laden with hot globes smacked me right on the side of the head.

The tumble had started; I was falling backwards into the crowd, and there was nothing I could do to stop myself. I wanted to laugh and say "Spook!", thinking of Iris doing exactly the same thing last week, but the pain wouldn't let me.

Anyway, someone was screaming and I couldn't concentrate.

Oh, it was *me*. . .

"Got you!" said Max, grabbing me hard around the waist, struggling to keep his balance in case we both went over.

"Jem! JEM!!" I heard Mum's voice call shrilly from somewhere close by. In the muddle of the moment, I saw Ben's concerned face in the crowd, but Max was now lowering me down into a bundle of waiting arms.

"Dad!" I called out feebly, recognizing him first in the haze of shock and pain because he was a) my dad, and b) a clown.

And apart from Mum's henna tattooed arms and Dad's padded white clown gloves reaching out to get me, another pair of hands seemed desperate to help.

The nails were pinky-white, like seashells.

The hands were delicate and birdlike.

The arms were covered in a grey-blue suit fabric.

The voice somehow connected to all this was familiar.

"Come here!" it said.

"*Excuse* me!" I heard my dad the clown say indignantly to the lady who was obviously from the council. "*I'll* see to this. She's *my* daughter!"

"Duh!" said the lady from the council in a

stunningly unprofessional voice. "I think I know *that*, Dad!"

As my head spun and whirled, I thought of butterflies and out-of-tune jewellery boxes and a whole mysterious trail of coincidences.

Everything went tangled and dark just seconds after I heard myself say, "I *knew* you were coming back, Gracie!"

And heard the sarcastic words, "Yeah, *right*, Jem!" in return.

(Blackness. . .)

Chapter 22

Totally cuckoo

Cuckoo!

Cuckoo!

As the seventh and eighth tweet rang out from the clock collection in the kitchen, Gracie smiled and rolled her eyes.

"Still a madhouse round here, then?" she said, as she pressed the bag of frozen peas against the side of my face.

You should have seen the place earlier, before the decorations were stripped down for the street party, I thought, wondering what she would have made of the permanent Christmas display, never mind the fact that it was all in her honour.

"You don't think she has concussion?" Mum was asking her.

"Nope – it wasn't her head that was hit, Mum."

"Are you *sure* we shouldn't we take Jem to the hospital?" Dad muttered worriedly, his clown face looming over me.

"Dad – I told you, she's *fine*. She just needs ice on that cheekbone for the swelling and rest for the shock."

It was the first thing we'd found out about her. Sometime in her unknown life my big sister had become a trained first-aider. What *else* were we going to discover about Gracie's secret world?

"Here, darling . . . sip on this," murmured Mum, passing me a glass of water that Viv had just fetched from the kitchen.

"So, you're Gracie, then?" Max asked out of the blue.

He was sitting on one of the armchairs in our living room, staring in fascination at the mythical creature perched on the sofa beside me. Ben was leaning against the back of the chair Iris had hobbled to, both of them as gobsmacked as if an *X-Factor* judge had just walked in the room. Viv and Ray were twittering around, not sure what to do or say or *think*, I suspected.

Though no one was as stunned as Mum and Dad, who were hovering either side of Gracie, looking as if they wanted to touch her, but acting like they were scared to, in case she was a mirage.

Then there was Dolly, plonked on my sister's very smart shoes, gazing intently into her face and trying terribly hard to recognize this oddly familiar person.

(Join the club, Dolly!)

"Well, *yes*, I'm Gracie," said Gracie, with a noticeable hint of her trademark sarcasm.

From where I was sitting – i.e., on the sofa with a packet of vegetables slightly blocking my view – she looked amazing. Amazingly grown-up, and amazingly beautiful, and amazingly amazing.

"Where have you *been*?" said Iris, blithely asking the question we all wanted to know the answer to.

(How weird, I thought, as I waited for Gracie to speak. *Outside*, the street party was carrying on, with giggles and shouts and laughter and dancing now that everybody knew that I was relatively OK. While *inside* 37 Priory Avenue, a small miracle was happening; the broken parts of a family were all together, even if they were just an uncertain jumble at the moment.)

"Brighton."

"Brighton?" said Ray, frowning at my sister. "But that's only about an hour and a half away, Gracie!

What were you doing there? Was that where the crowd from The Den ended up settling?!"

"What? *Nicko* and everyone*?!*" snorted Gracie, talking as if Ray had mentioned something silly and redundant from her childhood, like the Eeyore toy she'd once flung at my head. "God, *no*! I left them after a couple of months! All they did was just *talk* about stuff that was wrong in the world . . . they didn't actually *do* anything about it!"

"But I don't understand; if you *left* them, why didn't you come home, love?" Mum asked gently, as if she might be out of order to ask something so personal.

"Well, I suppose . . . I still wanted to try living my life *my* way," Gracie said, with a matter-of-fact shrug.

The shrug annoyed me. How could she be so casual when Mum and Dad had been out of their minds with sadness for so long? So much for the warm memories I'd had of her onstage. Maybe she *was* as brusque and self-centred as I remembered.

"Yeah, but what were you doing all this time, in your 'new life'?" I asked, struggling to get myself more upright and wriggling away from her hand and the ice pack.

Gracie looked slightly taken aback. I guess she'd left a useless, annoying little sister behind and not expected to find me all grown-up and full of attitude and logical questions.

"Well, my friend Jo felt the same way as me," she carried on calmly, firmly pressing the bag back on to my face, "so we left the guys from The Den behind, and went to stay with Jo's parents in Brighton for a bit. Then we both ended up going to college there, and I got a business diploma—"

"Good for you!" Dad interrupted, his clown smile wide and eager.

"—and now I work for a charity. I was just here today at a conference with my boss. I had a couple of hours to kill before we got the train back and I just thought—"

"How-whoo*OOOOO*!" Dolly took her turn to interrupt with a yodel. Stiffly, she clambered up into Gracie's lap, now that she'd matched this person on the sofa to the version of Gracie in her tattered memory banks.

"Aw, baby! When did you get so *old*!" Gracie cooed, in a voice that I vaguely remembered in my *own* tattered memory banks.

Wow, she was all softness again.

This was *such* emotional rollercoaster . . . a second ago I felt hugely angry with her, and here I was, with a brand new image in my head (of her helping me bury my darling hamster after next door's cat got its claws in him) and then a guilty thought slapped me around my already rattled head. Was I *always* poor, put-upon Jem? Or had I sometimes done a pretty good job of winding my sister up badly? By taking her stuff without asking? Taking the mickey in front of her friends? Taking her for granted?

"Dolly's just delighted to see you, same as all of us," said Mum, squatting down and tentatively putting her hand on Gracie's knee.

Gracie glanced up from Dolly, taking turns to look at the Henna Queen and Mr Wiggle, who just happened to be her loving, grateful parents, whether she liked it or not.

"Mum, Dad, I am one *hundred* per cent sorry if I hurt you, or worried you," she said, at last giving them the apology that they deserved. "It's just the longer I stayed away, the more sure I was that I wanted to, well, *prove* something to myself before I eventually came back."

"And *are* you back, Gracie?" Mum asked hopefully. "For good, I mean?"

"Oh, *no*!" Gracie shook her head, sounding absolutely like the old, self-centred girl who used to bug me. "I've got to go. . ."

She took the ice pack off my face – with a jangle of a bracelet with silver drops dangling from it – and checked her watch.

". . .*now*! My train's due soon, and there's not another one till morning."

Great. After more than two years, Gracie had waltzed into our lives – and she was about to waltz right back out.

"I'll drive you to the station. . ." said Dad.

"You will *not*, Owen!" Viv said firmly. "You've had a few beers today, remember. We *all* have. Ray, call a taxi for Gracie!"

Despite what Gracie-the-First-Aider had said, maybe I *did* have a slight concussion. Cause the next five minutes seemed to be a confusing jumble of hugs and snippets of explanations and jumbled descriptions and promises of contact that would be soon, soon, *soon* rather than much, much later. And all of this went on between Mum and Dad and Gracie, with the rest of us as dazed spectators. Even Dolly was more part of this reunion than me, with all the ear-rubbing going on.

Bring! Bring!

Ray picked up our house phone and found that the too-punctual taxi firm were already at the end of our closed-off road, waiting for their passenger.

"Bye then, Jem," Gracie said hesitantly, as she quit with her nursemaid duties and let me get to my feet.

"Er, mobile number," Max suddenly mumbled awkwardly, appearing between us, two sisters who didn't know what to say to each other.

He was holding out the spook book to Gracie, with a pen he must've got from Iris too.

"You'll have to go now if you want to catch your train," Ray urged Gracie, hurrying her as she scribbled down her number on the pad.

For the merest second, our eyes met, and then she was gone, with Mum and Dad hugging her like a pair of protective octopuses as they rushed down the road with her to the waiting taxi.

"I'm going upstairs," I muttered to whoever was left in the room.

Ben and Max and even Iris on her crutches got up as if they were going to follow me, but I put a stop to it with the addition of the word "*alone*".

Someone *did* tag along, though. Because she

wasn't too hot on words any more, Dolly ignored what I'd just said and trotted awkwardly behind me as I leapt up the stairs, two at a time, and barged into Gracie's room.

"What was the *point*?" I turned to Dolly and asked despairingly, as I grabbed the music box and slouched on Gracie's window sill. "What were all the signs and the spooks for if that's *it*?!?"

A few minutes ago, I'd been thinking small miracles and mended families, but now – as I gazed down at the ongoing street party – all I could feel was disappointment.

Perhaps, of course, this was my punishment for the wish I'd kept secret all this time.

Actually . . . Max and Iris might have thought what I said was no big deal, but I needed to hear it from Gracie *herself*.

My chest tight with nerves, I took the rolled-up spook book out of my pocket, found the number Max had made Gracie scribble down and nervously tapped it in.

It rang.

She picked up.

Help.

"Hello?"

"Gracie – it's me," I said, my heart pitter-patter-pounding. "Jem."

"Oh. Hey, Jem. You're going to have to speak louder; I'm in the cab and I can't hear too well with the traffic."

I couldn't hear her too well either; not with Dolly yodelling along to the music that was drifting in from the party outside. (And outside at the party, I could see Mum and Dad, animatedly chatting to neighbours, spilling the good news of the long-lost daughter found.)

"I need to ask you something," I began.

"Shoot," replied Gracie, in that dead-straight way of hers.

Here I go, I thought, hoping I'd still be able to breathe.

"Did you leave because of me?"

I heard an incredulous snort of laughter.

"*Why* would I leave because of you, Jem?"

"Because of what I said. . ."

"What? What did you say?" she asked, sounding far away and confused.

"It was at the drumming concert you took me to. I said I wished you'd leave."

As I spoke, my eyes settled now on Ben down

below, hunched on the edge of the stage, biting his nails and looking concerned. Max was with him, discussing our family drama, I supposed.

"Jem, I can't even *remember* that! I probably wasn't even listening properly. I was too busy that day with all the planning and packing I had to do in secret."

"Huh? So . . . so you already *knew* you were going then?" I said, relief instantly flooding every vein.

"Well, yes, of course! I wouldn't be so stupid as to take off just cause my kid sister came out with something dumb!"

OK. So if it really, *definitely* wasn't to do with me, was it to do with someone *else*?

"Gracie, did you leave cause of. . ." I hesitated, trying to clear something else up. ". . .because of Spike?"

There was the faintest pause, and then a tinkling clunk, as if something – the bracelet with the silvery stones? – was banging up against the phone.

"Listen, I didn't go just because of Spike," Gracie said at last. "Well, maybe a little bit. . . Wow, was I mad about him back then. Oh no – I just thought of something."

"What?"

"I wrote him this *awful*, *gushy* goodbye letter. I was even going to put a little present in with it – a wristband! Thank God I never sent it. I'd have been so embarrassed if he'd got that. . ."

Oops. I hoped Gracie couldn't hear me gulp.

"But anyway, Jem, I just left because I was unhappy and restless and needed to go. I wanted to see what was out there."

"And what *was* out there?" I asked her, pressing my head to the cool window, feeling Dolly's wet nose nuzzle my hand.

I vaguely noticed that Dad had come up to Max now, and was chatting and patting him warmly on the back, while Max nodded and grinned. Ah – I had an idea that I might just know who Dad's next apprentice clown would be. . .

"Good stuff, bad stuff, interesting stuff," Gracie replied. "I'll tell you all about it sometime, Jem. But not today – I mean, I didn't even know I was going to come and see you all. It was honestly just a spur of the moment thing."

"No it wasn't – I knew you were on your way back!" I contradicted her, not really caring if Gracie believed me or not. "There were *way* too many signs and coincidences, like your jewellery box playing in the middle of the night and then these butterflies that I kept see—"

"Jemima Wisniewski – still as superstitious as ever!" she interrupted me with a laugh.

"Gracie Wisniewski – still as cynical as ever!" I joked back, relieved to smile now that all the secrets were out in the open.

"Er, it's Gracie Rodgers, actually."

Or maybe they weren't.

"You changed your *name*?" I asked her, shocked.

"Well, yeah. I got married. Last year. To my friend – the one I went to stay with in Brighton."

"Jo?!?" I blurted out, rocked from this tsunami of news.

"Yeah, Joe – the guy I got to know from The Den. Like I say, we were just friends for a long time and then we—"

"What!?!" I yelped, taking my turn to interrupt her. "Jo is a *Joe*, and you *married* him? When did you plan on telling us *that* tiny detail?"

"Jem, I didn't want to blast Mum and Dad with everything at once. They seemed pretty shell-shocked as it was. Please don't tell them – I'll come back for a proper visit soon, and I'll let them know then, I promise!"

"But—" I began to protest, not keen on suddenly being in charge of another hefty secret so soon after offloading the last one.

"Look, I've got to go – the taxi's just pulling into the station and I can see my boss. We'll talk later, yeah?"

"OK," I mumbled, not quite ready to say goodbye yet to this frustrating, complicated, interesting girl I happened to be related to.

"Oh, and one last thing, Jem – I loved that corny old music box you bought me. But you DIDN'T hear it play, because it was cheap and useless and never worked!"

And with that she was gone, the sister who'd only just arrived.

I looked down into Dolly's squinty little eyes and murmured, "She's wrong, isn't she? We *both* heard it play!"

I sprang open the lid and wound up the key at the back of the box, waiting for the too-fast plinking to begin, for the tatty plastic doll to spin around.

Nothing.

I tried again. And again.

Nothing.

Spook! Or maybe *no more* spooks. Maybe this was finally the end of my summer of strangeness and signs?

Now that Gracie had come back into our lives, my own life could get back to normal. I'd just be Jem, the goofy girl who occasionally whacked herself on the back of the head with her guitar. Jem, who might one of these days be the girlfriend of someone called Ben. . . (Cue my tummy doing a back flip at the very thought.)

With a shiver, I snapped the music box lid shut and gazed back down to the party scene below. The stage was illuminated once again, I noticed, not by fairy lights this time (of course) but by our trio of the singing snowman, the reindeer and the hunched Santa Claus.

In front of them was a *marginally* less nuts-looking trio – Iris had hobbled out to join the boys. I pushed the window open to feel the cool breeze on my hot and swollen face.

"Hey, Jem!" Iris called out, waving her tinsel-covered crutch.

Ben – beautiful Ben – turned and smiled up at me (yep, another back flip; *double* this time).

Meanwhile, Max – stupid, kind, fuzzy Max with his smudged white face paint – gave a whoop, then jumped onstage, landing right beside the snowman.

"Oi! Jem!" he yelled, as the snowman's sensor went off and it began its familiar wobbling dance. "Check out my *moves*!!"

And with his ridiculous matching wobbly dance – and those six little words – I suddenly knew I'd found out one *last* secret.

Me and Gracie shared something *else* in common: the same taste in cute, dorky boys. Hers was called Spike (and now Joe, maybe?), and mine . . . mine was called *Max*.

Max, my goofy knight in furry armour, always there to make me laugh, stop me stage-diving when I didn't mean to, and hold fingers with me in unexpected situations. (Sorry, Ben – I just realized the tummy flips were all about me cringing with awkwardness, cause I didn't feel the same way back.)

And although I thought I was all done with wishes, maybe I had *one* more in me.

"I wish . . . I wish that Max would like me as much as I like him!" I whispered, crossing my fingers tight, tight, tight.

"Harumpppph!" Dolly sighed, while happily settling herself on my shoes, as if that was the *best* idea she'd heard all day.

"*Plink!*" came a little discordant note from a closed music box that wasn't supposed to work.

I took both sounds to be a very, *very* good sign indeed. . .